BRIGHT BLUE
Miracle

A Novel By

BECCA WILHITE

**SHADOW
MOUNTAIN**®

For the remarkable Becky Jackson,
my lovely steptwin.
This story is not *about you.*

Library of Congress Cataloging-in-Publication Data

Wilhite, Becca.
    Bright blue miracle / Becca Wilhite.
        p. cm.
    Summary: Seventeen-year-old Leigh feels jealous when her best friend
Jeremy starts to date Leigh's new stepsister.
    ISBN 978-1-60641-031-8 (paperbound)
    [1. Best friends—Fiction.   2. Friendship—Fiction.
3. Stepsisters—Fiction.]   I. Title.
    PZ7.W64825Br 2009
    [Fic]—dc22   2008035764

Printed in the United States of America
Publishers Printing, Salt Lake City, UT

10   9   8   7   6   5   4   3   2   1

Chapter 1

When you're seventeen, your best friend is supposed to be the one you giggle with and watch sad movies with—the kind that make you both cry. You're supposed to have sleepovers at each other's houses and secretly eat an entire bag of potato chips before breakfast. You're supposed to be able to share the combination of excitement and revulsion that comes over you as your body becomes something distinct from a thirteen-year-old boy's. You're supposed to trade clothes and have crushes on the same guy and feel excited for each other when there's the possibility of a date for the prom. You should write each other notes and tape them in your shared locker.

Well, just like so many things that don't turn out the way they're supposed to, my best friend and I are nothing like that. My best friend does not cry in sad movies, rarely writes notes, and has possibly never giggled. Sleepovers are out of the question, and, frankly, discussions about the changes in our bodies are few and awkward. My best friend is not a girly-girl, a smart girl, a pretty girl, or any kind of girl. My best friend is Jeremy Bentley, lovingly referred to around my house as "Germ."

We met in seventh grade, as awkward a time in my life as you'd imagine. Jeremy was this tall, gangly kid with brown hair that flopped down over his glasses. We were in the same civics class, and I was pleased and surprised to discover that this kid who always seemed to need a haircut was, in fact, a budding social psychologist.

With a perspective on every issue, you'd think he'd get annoying in class, but he never volunteered his theories. Mrs. Oaks made us write a paragraph in response to a news item of her choice every day, and would generally read Jeremy's aloud. She never told us who wrote the papers she read, but it became clear that there were few thirteen-year-olds who could make a reasonably intelligent statement about homeless shelters or famine or socialized medicine or the Ebola virus before 8:30 in the morning.

Half the class would sit staring dumbly at Mrs. Oaks as she'd read what she called "a nugget of insight from one of our little Acorns"—which was, of course, to remind us that we all had the potential to become Mighty Oaks, just like she was. Watching a deep red blush creep up from Jeremy's shirt collar, I caught myself blushing too. It was somehow embarrassing to me that his insights were being wasted on the likes of Drew Miller (if there wasn't a football in the story, there had better be a basketball) and Penny "my-life's-goal-is-to-retain-my-nineteen-inch-waist" Goldman.

When Jeremy and I got paired up to report on the effect of an illness on a culture, I was secretly pleased to have a chance to pick his brain, and I was not disappointed. For two weeks we worked on what turned out to be a great report on the bubonic plague in Europe. My dad taught at the university and he helped us locate great research sources and pronounce names like *Camus*. We even made a repulsively lifelike boil to lance for the class, and we borrowed Jeremy's cousin's pet rat for a visual aid.

It was completely bizarre and fabulous to meet someone who liked to hang out in the library or ride the bus to the university just to sit in my dad's office and plan a recipe for blister pus. This kind of shy, slightly awkward, tall kid was as cool as they come. On the day of the reports, Penny Goldman walked into class in her older sister's cheerleading uniform and reported a "shocking and disturbing" outbreak of mono in the high school, the effect of which was to shake the entire dating structure: "My sister is, like, totally afraid to kiss anybody now." Jeremy was practically under his desk laughing, and I knew I had found the friend I was waiting for.

And now for years, even through some rough times, we'd been great. We had fun together. Life was good. I'd made it over most of the major hurdles you'd expect, and a couple I had never expected. I was in the flow and didn't need any more character-building experiences to give me depth. I wasn't asking for anything new or different or even interesting. But apparently what I wanted didn't matter. Because new and different and maybe even interesting was all headed my way. Right into my house, ready or not.

Is it possible for two very nice, adequately good-looking, and fairly intelligent people to embark on a doomed marriage? Consider it likely when they each have a teenage daughter.

Blended family. Could there be a more disgusting image? Take a handful of these guys and add a handful of those guys, chuck them in a jar, Do Not Operate Without Lid In

Place, and push the button. Mmmm. Yeah. Who wouldn't want to get in on that? And there's no better recipe for removing any interesting personal details and character traits than throwing everything in the blender. Of all the things I hoped for in my years on this planet, being frappéed was never near the top of the list. But when Christmas rolled around, Mom handed me an emotional blender.

I tend to get nervous when Mom oversells something. A trust-me-you'll-love-it comment is always more convincing than a lengthy list of reasons to give something a chance, which is why I felt wary about Elisabeth from the get-go.

"Paul has a daughter. She's about your age." That would have been enough. I'd have formed an unbiased opinion starting from those basics. But no. To insure my unwavering interest in Paul Burke's daughter, I was subjected to detail after frightful detail. "She plays tennis and the piano. She's read lots of the books you like. Her hair is exactly the color of clover honey. She grew up in the mountains and loves to hike. Did I mention how pretty she is? She has the most engaging features. She's very smart, but seems rather shy." Blah, blah-blah, blah-blah.

Apparently Mom wasn't aware that I'd stopped being an active participant in this litany of Elisabeth's virtues. Talking to a gerbil, she'd have gotten more response. Until this: "Betsy's never been to Indianapolis. Even though she's anxious to come visit, she's nervous."

"Who?"

"Leigh, who do you think we've been talking about? Elisabeth." She looked sideways at me, letting me know I had displeased her.

"Sorry. I thought you said Betsy."

"Elisabeth *is* Betsy."

Betsy. Was she kidding? Betsy Burke? How could anyone with a particle of self-respect run around as *Betsy Burke?* I stifled a laugh and managed a noncommittal noise of understanding.

"Look, Leigh. I know you're keeping yourself distant from Paul, and I understand that—but do this for me. Get to know Betsy. Give her a try. You both deserve to make this work."

"Make what work? My mother is long-distance dating her father. We happen to live on different sides of the Mississippi River, and that's not likely to change anytime soon. It's not like you and Paul are planning anything ridiculous like getting married."

What I would call a lengthy and uncomfortable silence fell at this point.

Then I saw my own mother blush.

Beginning to feel sick to my stomach, I muttered, "Mom? What terribly important, possibly crucial detail of your plans for my future have you neglected to tell me about?"

"Sweetie, we wanted to wait till Paul and Betsy were here to discuss this. You know, kind of a family council."

I was so close to actually throwing up that I had to put my head down.

"I guess there's no use putting it off now. Paul and I have decided to get married. I'd like to know how you feel about that, but if you'd rather not talk about it now, I understand."

No response.

"I'd prefer it if you didn't talk to the twins about this just yet, okay? I don't think they're ready for this news."

Like I was? So she'd like to know how I felt. *She'd like to know how I felt?* I'd love to have had the words to define the mixture of shock, revulsion, betrayal, and my impending mutiny.

Merry Christmas.

———

Mom decided that waiting for The Visit to tell the twins about the engagement might be a dumb idea. She had learned not to trust me to keep a secret, which was only fair, I'm afraid. Not that I don't enjoy suspense as much as the next girl, I just hate being out of the loop. So I may have threatened just a little to let the twins in on the Very Big News if she didn't go ahead and tell them what she and Paul had planned.

There we sat, passing green beans and salad around the dinner table, when out of Mom's lovely mouth came these words: "Hey, Emily and Sarah, how would you like to have a bigger family?"

Struggling not to choke, I managed, "Objection, Your Honor. Leading the witnesses."

Mom grinned, overruled my objection, and gave the twins her full attention (translation: *ignored me*—of course).

Emily looked thoughtful. She forked several green beans in a pile and asked, "Are you going to have a baby?"

Mom kept a straight face, dug a handful of fingernails into my forearm to prevent my input, and replied, "No, honey. A woman ought to be married to have a baby. I'm not married since Daddy died."

"Well, there are those who would disagree . . ." I tried. Yikes, the fingernails. I took the gentle hint and shut up.

"So maybe you should get married again," Sarah said. "That could be a good idea, you know."

Mom smiled. "Do you think so, love? Why? How come it would be a good thing for me to marry someone?"

Sarah shrugged and reached for the salad dressing. "Leigh wouldn't have to kill the spiders."

"Or," Emily added, "empty the mousetraps. That seems like a husband's job, Mom. And maybe he could mow the lawn. And fix the shower drip. And open those big pickle jars. And build stuff. And—"

Mom interrupted her, "Emmy, we're not talking about hiring a handyman, okay? Avoiding unpleasant jobs is not a very good reason to marry someone."

"Well," Sarah wanted to know, "what is a good reason?"

Mom sighed and smiled in a fairly sickening manner. "Love, baby. If you love someone, that's a good reason for doing lots of things."

I could not keep it in any longer. If I didn't speak now, I would definitely regret it. Or throw up. Or both. "But isn't loving someone—or lots of someones—also a good reason to avoid some things? Like wrecking their lives? Like throwing their happiness in the toilet? Like setting them up for rejection and adding totally needless complications to their families?"

Mom looked sad and stern at the same time. "Leigh, I would appreciate you not making this difficult. More difficult. Please. Smarten up or excuse yourself."

I hadn't heard her talk to me like that for a long time. We had mostly gotten past the period in my life where I needed a lot of correcting. It should have given me a driving sense of my stupidity and guilt, but instead, I decided to quit the sugar-coating and tell her how I really felt.

"You would not like *me* to make this difficult for *you?* Well, guess what? I would have really appreciated it if you had not made everything hard for me. Starting with inviting Paul and Betsy to our house and into our family. Especially at Christmas. We don't need them. We have plenty of kids in this family. Three is a lot of kids. And we don't need a replacement father. We loved Dad enough to just be happy remembering him. If you'd loved him enough, you wouldn't run right out and marry the first guy you came across." Hearing myself say those words shocked me, but I was on a roll and not about to stop.

"You don't really care what Emily and Sarah and I think about your plans. You're just going to go ahead and do whatever you feel like anyway, so stop acting like this is some sort of family decision. Just put it all out on the table. You're going to marry Paul. He's going to move into our house. He's going to act like he's our father. His perfect daughter is going to show us all what we should be like and mock us for being talentless and short. They're going to take down our family pictures and bring in their own, and they'll try to erase our dad from our house and our lives." My voice was rising dangerously. I could feel the blood pulsing behind my eyeballs. If I didn't let this out, my head would surely explode.

"If you had cared what we thought, you'd have brought this up earlier, not two days before they show up to spend Christmas with us. You didn't tell us before because you didn't want to hear the truth. We. Don't. Want. Paul. Or. Betsy. We are fine. We are family enough. You don't need to fix us. Paul Burke should just stay away from here and leave us alone."

My last few words seemed to echo through the kitchen. I realized I was standing in front of my overturned chair holding a serving spoon. Yelling. I had been yelling. At my mom. In front of my little sisters. Not a yeller by nature or habit, I finally shocked myself into silence. Looking at Mom and the twins, I realized they were all crying. Slowly I set down the spoon and raised my hand to my mouth. I stared at my mom, willing her to see my apology in my eyes.

She reached over and righted my chair. Taking my hand, she pulled me down onto it.

"Leigh." Weighty pause, as if counting to ten. "That was a lot to say. You have every right to feel those feelings, and to express them. But your tone is unacceptable, and in order to be fair, you should not speak for the twins. They will be allowed to say what they need to say without your help. I will give them a chance to speak in a second, but first, is there anything else you need to say right now?"

She was glaring at me meaningfully.

Several events and decisions over the last few years could be stacked neatly into the category of Being a Good Example. This fit perfectly, and I decided to swallow my anger, my pride, and a glass full of water. Then I managed, "I'm very sorry that I shouted. I should have chosen to excuse myself. Please forgive me, Mom. I'm sorry, Em. Sorry, Sarah."

"Thank you." Mom tried to look like she didn't want to reach over and smack me. She took a deep breath and gave us a shaky smile. The twins were still crying into their plates.

"Well, girls, I think we should try this again," Mom began.

"I have some very big news to tell you. Paul and I have decided to get married, and he and his daughter are coming to live with us. But first, they will come to visit for Christmas, and I hope all of you will do your very best to make them feel at home. Paul already knows how wonderful you all are, and I'm sure you'll just love Elisabeth. Does anyone have anything to say right now?"

Mom was on a roll, leading us to be emotionally open and healthy, ready to validate us, and all that. Please, someone shoot me if I ever sign up for a psychology class.

"I like our family. I think we're nice. I think Paul's nice too. He's a good match." Emily nodded with first-grade finality.

Sarah nodded as well. "And it's going to be great for Leigh to have a twin. Having a twin is my favorite." She smiled through what remained of her tears and wiped her runny, freckled nose on a linen napkin.

I smiled back at her and, with my hand on my heart, said, "I solemnly promise and vow to be as pleasant, as friendly, and as gracious as I can about our new arrangement. I will do my best to be a team player." Teamwork was big in the Mason family. We each put a hand in and made a stack.

"Goooooo, Masons!" we all cheered.

Chapter 2

There's something about me I've discovered—a defective part. I appear to have been born without a filter. When something pops into my head, it generally pops right out of my mouth. This has, as you may imagine, moderate to serious consequences in a family scenario. Without preamble, I am likely to blurt, "Mom, you realize you are the twenty-first-century equivalent of a mail-order bride, right? Internet wife." I wished Jeremy had been around to hear that. He'd have laughed. A thousand curses upon out-of-town Christmas vacations.

Emily perked up in the back seat. "What's a mail-order bride?" she wanted to know.

"Back in the old days, a farmer would work his wife to death digging and planting and milking cows and making babies. Then he'd need a new wife, so he'd write a little letter, reporting that he was tall and handsome and wealthy and generally fabulous, and some trusting soul would believe it. Then she'd write her own letter (or have someone who could write do it for her), detailing all of her virtues, real or imagined, not forgetting child-bearing hips, and they'd seal the deal. She'd get a train ticket, and he'd get a whole new wife. Presto, like magic." I waved my fingers like a magician with a wand.

Sarah grimaced. "Like getting books from Amazon? Gross. What if he didn't like her? What if she was . . . gruesome?"

"Excellent word, Sarah-Bear. I guess too bad if she was. No return policy. Just a chance you take when you order." I was really warming up to this topic, but I noticed Mom's uncharacteristically tight hold on the steering wheel so I attempted to lighten up. "No worries here, though. Mom's beautiful, right? And Paul is almost as handsome as his Internet photo made him look. Besides, we've liked him well enough both times he's been here. No gruesome people here. Well," I added after a thoughtful pause, "except for us." I pulled the most frightful faces over the back of my seat, sending Emily and Sarah into hysterics.

As promised, I put on my happy face for Paul's and his flawless daughter's arrival. As Mom parked at the meter, I wandered with the twins into the overdecorated airport lobby. All the security arrangements gave me the chance to scan the arrivals en masse. Eenie, meenie, miney, mo. I picked out this (honestly) geeky-looking girl to be Betsy, but no luck. She was clearly traveling with her nearly identical geeky mother.

Fixing on some very pretty hair, I waited for another girl to turn around, only to be surprised that she was a guy. Eww. Automatically gotta hate the boys with more feminine features than mine. Next? Here came a dad, but he was lugging a sleeping toddler and motivating a tired preschooler with his gentle foot. I gave them a sympathetic smile at the baggage claim and turned to face my future. My leggy, tanned, white-toothed, and exceptionally pretty new family. Smiling like a toothpaste ad. Wearing ski parkas. To Indiana. Come on, who were they trying to kid?

Right there in the lobby I felt myself shrink two inches (which I could ill afford). Paul smiled down at me and showed equally fantastic teeth. Great. They were legitimate. I had forgotten that part of his handsome face. Denied the privilege of sneering at cosmetic dentistry, I held out my hand to Paul. He gave the expected half-hug with his other arm, high-fived the twins, and turned me again in Betsy's direction. She wasn't getting any uglier standing in the airport. Short, polite introduction behind us, we all began the process of becoming a family. Sigh.

Double-buckling the twins into the Accord, Betsy and I squeezed in beside them. Part of my "happy face" agreement was the understanding that I was under no circumstances to complain about automotive safety issues. Check.

Mom had insisted on waiting to decorate the tree until the infiltrators—I mean *company*—arrived, so our house was the only one on the street without twinkle lights. As we pulled into the driveway, I tried to see our home through strangers' eyes. Frankly, it couldn't have been much less impressive. Gray, bare trees; gray shingles; gray ivy twigs clinging to the gray paint; gray sticks of shrubs; gray, icy snow schmutz lumped along the sidewalk.

"It's much prettier in the spring," I found myself telling Betsy and Paul. Why should I care if they were impressed? But I did care. I wanted to give them nothing to hold against us. The Burkes gave me a pair of their bright, even smiles. Oh, how I wanted to throw up.

The Burkes. We were about to become a group known as

the Burkes. But *we* weren't Burkes. We were The Other Kids. From now on Sarah, Emily, and I would be known as The First Husband's Kids. In a matter of weeks, there would be no more Mason family. Just the Burke Family and The Other Kids.

———

Christmas was the most careful affair I'd ever experienced. As a group, we questioned everything. Where should we put the tree? (Obviously in the bay window, where it always goes.) When should we put up lights? (Last month, but too bad.) What should we eat for dinner, and should our big meal be on Christmas Eve, or Christmas Day? No tradition was taken for granted. We were trying so hard to act like a brand-spanking-new family.

Paul and Betsy had a new-pajama tradition they thought we should get in on, so we all trooped over to the mall on the most ridiculous shopping day of the year and bought each other new jammies. The Burkes had never had our traditional scones for Christmas Eve dinner, so they tried out a meal made up solely of carbs and cooking oil. We were all pleasant enough, with the result that the entire week felt like a too-long first date. You know, wear your pleasant smile, keep your controversial opinions to yourself, be willing to try new things (within reason), heave an enormous deep breath when it's over.

I guess the main difference between our "first date" and a real first date was the sleeping arrangements. Paul slept on the basement couch. If we'd had nosy neighbors, Mom would probably have insisted on chastely sending him to a hotel. But our neighbors were not at all the nosy kind, though I did catch Mrs.

Daines doing a double take when Paul took out the trash. It seemed like she was sort of checking him out, which is gross because she's like sixty. So Paul slept in the basement on the couch and Betsy had the living room. Sarah and Emily invited her to share their bunks, but she passed. Our family's first date just went on and on, with me sleeping in as late in the mornings as I could, killing "together time" the best way I knew how.

I'm not sure what I was thinking. Had I imagined that the couch-sleeping scenario would last forever? I really hated to think of Paul moving into my mother's room, so I just refused to consider it. But how had I missed the decision that Betsy would share my room? Maybe Mom had thought it would be a good idea to avoid discussing it. Maybe she thought I'd love the plan—a built-in twin! And in my room! What could possibly be more fun? Maybe, since there were no alternatives, she could see that I'd just have to buck up and deal with it. That was the most likely. Whatever the reason, I didn't actually think too much about the possibility of sharing a bedroom with a perfect stranger. Emphasis on *perfect*.

I managed to avoid seeing my mother kiss Paul Burke until we dropped them at the airport. My guts twisted to see her in his arms, but I was being very open-minded and grown-up about her marrying anyone who was not my dad, since my dad was irreversibly out of the picture. It was time for her to move on. It was just too bad that we all had to move on with her.

⌒

Weddings have never really held any fascination for me. I have no gown sketches or floral ads tucked beneath my pillow.

I guess I'm just not the kind of girl who names her children a decade before they're born, either. Don't get me wrong. I'm in favor of marriage. I just don't think too much about the wedding part of it.

But I'm always up for a party, and where there is food, there is fun. I agreed to help Mom plan her soirée (because parties, like all other things, increase in class when spoken in French). My only demand was that it not be too close to Valentine's Day because . . . well, eww. So we put one of Emily's heart stickers on the calendar for January 19th and I persevered.

After Paul and Betsy hustled back to Denver in preparation for The Big Move, Jeremy found his way back to my house. Spending his Christmas vacations in Utah with his grandparents (both sets) was a long-standing tradition, and he had the standard sunburned nose of a ski bum. As we sat at the table peeling and sticking address labels on postcards, Jeremy turned one over.

"Hey. Do I get one of these? This is a great picture of you." The photo side of the postcard was The Family: Paul, Mom, Betsy, the twins, and me.

"Yeah, I'm sure your family's on the list. If not, I'll get one blown up life-sized for your viewing pleasure. You can mount it on your bedroom ceiling and stare at it while you try to get to sleep."

Still studying the photo, Jeremy was falling behind on his sticking duties. "Oy," I grumbled, waving my hand covered with label stickers. "I've got no more fingers."

"Mmm. Okay. Sorry," he said distractedly, beginning again

to affix addresses to the other side of the cards. I noticed, however, that he was still glancing at the photo. Kind of a lot.

"Hey, guess what? Real thing, right here."

"Yeah, but I wasn't looking at you . . . only."

"Nice cover. No, really." I heaved a drama queen sigh.

"She looks pretty."

Why deny it? "She is pretty, Germ. See how that picture makes me look roughly thirty percent better than usual? Some mathematical formula only you would understand could explain this, but she's actually thirty, maybe thirty-five percent better-looking than this photo makes her. It's like we magically met in the middle for a decent shot."

"Huh."

"Yeah, okay. Time to switch. You peel. I'll stick." I grabbed the pile of finished cards and tossed them into the bin. He turned over a new one to the photo side.

~

Imagine my delight when Mom agreed that the ska band Skates for Jake was the best we'd auditioned for the reception. This was an unexpected bonus. Between moments of overbearing emotional displays from current and future relatives, I would get to dance. Jeremy was acting noncommittal about the whole reception thing because he's sort of an awkward dancer. But I knew he would come to the party for the crab claws and spinach dip.

Yoga-breathing through the ceremony kept my mind clear of unpleasant and possibly impure thoughts of what was ahead. It was best to let the "later" part stay unexplored. Betsy was, in fairness, trying not to crowd me during the reception. Mom's request (read: *demand*) that I keep Miss Elisabeth amused and entertained through the evening weighed on me. But I had made an effort, and it wasn't going too badly. Without a sense that the foundation of my life was about to crumble, I saw Jeremy wander in the door and waved him over.

"Hey, Germ. It's about time you showed up. We were just starting to think we'd have to entertain each other all night. Betsy Burke, this is Jeremy Bentley. Jeremy, Betsy."

She looked nervous and not at all sure what to do with her hands. Jeremy waved and smiled. "Betsy, I'm happy to meet you. Leigh has told me so much about you. Welcome to Indianapolis."

Oh, brother. *So much about you? Like what? She's prettier than her picture? Give me a break.* What could I have told? Even after all the small talk of one Christmas vacation plus a day and a half of wedding business, I knew just about nothing at all. Maybe I should have felt troubled by that. Or not.

Acting his normal, abnormally courteous self, Jeremy put Elisabeth at ease. There was music; there should be dancing. Taking each of us by a hand, Jeremy pulled us out of our chairs and onto the dance floor. Yeah, he was not a great dancer, but he was fun, and we were laughing at his graceless attempts to amuse us with his moves. Everything was fine, until the next song. It had a distinctly slower beat. I saw them look at each other and do a shy-smile thing, and Jeremy asked me if I minded if he danced with Betsy.

"Well, I wasn't going to ask her," I laughed, still alarmingly clueless.

I danced once with Paul and once with his much-younger

brother who was frighteningly not so much older than me. Feeling relieved that he was less handsome than Paul, I thanked him and bolted away when the song was over. I was very much not interested in getting interested, you know? Especially in anyone who had even a tenuous family connection. Finding Jeremy and Betsy again, I suggested a round of reception punch, which turned out to be a strange pinkish color not directly connected to any known fruit. We were each charming in our own ways. We laughed, we ate, we drank whatever that was. The three of us sat at a table and, as we talked, I allowed myself to believe this could work out just fine.

⌒

The Honeymoon. The less said, the better. A long weekend spent confined to the house with the twins. And Betsy.

Here are the things I discovered about Miss Betsy in that weekend:

She can make very good food out of pantry items and onions.

She likes to use her headphones so we don't all have to hear her music.

She makes her bed as soon as she gets out of it.

She rinses out the sink after tooth-brushing.

She didn't get her good hair from 100 strokes at night. Minimal primping.

She didn't get a phone call from her mom. And I never saw her make a call, either.

She makes herself useful and then makes herself scarce.

She hasn't seen the last several years' worth of animated kid movies.

She keeps a journal.

She seems more comfortable moving into my house than I would be moving into hers.

Upon the return of the newlyweds (shudder), life shifted into the new normal. School, meals at the big table, home-work, watching the mailbox for college acceptance letters, hanging with The Family.

For the few weeks after the wedding I made a glorious effort to please Mom. I invited Betsy to help pick out movies and play games. I showed her around school, I introduced her to friends, and I basically let her hang out everywhere I was. After two weeks, that got old.

Jeremy found his place in the mix, and because he was just that kind of guy, he fit into the new arrangement much more smoothly than I did. He acted like it was no big deal to have another body at the table, on the couch, or in the car. He asked polite questions and actually seemed interested in the answers.

Betsy, Jeremy, and I were playing Boggle on a Saturday afternoon. I was kicking their chicken, as my dad used to say. Finding perverse pleasure in untangling words like *unwanted* and *disaster* and *crowded* in consecutive rounds, I was warm-ing up to this companionship. If nothing else, their words made mine look brilliant. After a long string of three- and four-letter words, Betsy was obviously ready to call it a day.

"Let's go somewhere. What's your favorite place to hang out?" she asked, looking (I thought) fairly obviously at Jeremy.

Thoughtful as always, Germ was taking his time to answer,

whereas I was ready with a smart response. "We love the paddleboats on the canal downtown. Too bad they're two-seaters."

Jeremy shot me a glare. I raised my eyebrows in an effort to look innocent. He said, "It's the first week in February. The canal doesn't seem too inviting. What about a game of tennis? I could call my cousin to make four." Smiling at both of us, Jeremy began to look like he meant it. Mentally I ran through my list of excuses without finding an appropriate one. Besides the old standby, that I couldn't hit a tennis ball that was aimed perfectly at my navel.

"I love tennis! That would be excellent," Betsy grinned. Oh, those teeth made my stomach hurt.

Jeremy smiled back and phoned the cousin of rat fame. He was a nice guy, but . . . yeah. He had a rat. 'Nuff said. Then he phoned some doctor friend he knew from his church or something who happened to have a covered court on his property, and just like that, we had a plan.

I jumped in the front seat of Jeremy's car without even thinking. After all, why should I have to think about it? That was my place. Jeremy opened the back door for Betsy. Sliding all the way to the middle, she buckled her seat belt and smiled sweetly. "Thanks for always driving, Jeremy. You're saving us a fortune in gas. Leigh never drives. I haven't seen her behind the wheel once since I've been here. That Jeep must get lonely parked out in that garage all the time."

I stared in horror at the windshield. Was she kidding? Was she ignorant? Was she *mean?* With no idea how to respond, I just shook my head. Over and over. For a long time. Like someone in an advanced state of shock. I felt Jeremy's hand on my knee bringing me back to sense as he answered Betsy.

"No big thing. I like to drive. Maybe it's some latent macho-image gene making itself obvious. And, you know, it's kind of icy." He squeezed my knee and we were off to pick up Rat Guy. Jeremy watched Betsy in his mirror throughout the entire drive. If I hadn't been seated directly beside him, I may have worried that he'd forgotten I was there.

Heading out to the tennis house, I watched a couple of cardinals darting through the trees branching over the road, their red wings flashing through the black limbs. This was such a great spot in the summer. On sweltering August afternoons the trees held the coolness of the shade so well, you almost missed the humidity for a few minutes.

"My dad used to love to ride his bike out here." Did I say that out loud? Shoot. I meant to hold a grudging silence against Betsy's intrusive insensitivity. She did an interested "hmm" noise and I let it drop. After everything else we were sharing now, I planned to keep my dad to myself.

Rat Guy was thrilled to play on Betsy's team. He seemed way more interested in her than in the game. He kept calling her "partner," à la John Wayne. Ick. I was even starting to feel sorry for her, just a little. Jeremy was working the court, making up for my lack of playing ability. Twice I hit the ball directly over the net. Once, Betsy backhanded it right back to me, scaring me silly. I watched it bounce eighteen inches in front of me and on over the line. I shrugged my "sorry," and Germ grinned. What a guy—he had no pride.

After the match, I was so done. But Betsy suggested

playing boys against girls. I think she was a little tired of cowboy high-fives.

"You saw me play, right? So you are aware that we're about to get clobbered? There is a law of geophysics that explains why I can never hit a moving object," I whined.

Betsy shrugged. "Maybe I can just make up for you. This time, I'll turn it on," she whispered with a grin. I don't know if she was trying to make herself likable, but I had already determined it wouldn't work, thank you very much.

Turned out she didn't need me. Her arms were everywhere. She took on those two guys like they were nothing. Rarely have I seen anything like it—because I don't watch tennis. Ever. But she was amazing. I sort of galloped from one side of the backcourt to the other, pretty much staying out of her way. Every time our team scored, she cheered at me as though I'd had something to do with it. But my serves went over the net without escaping the court, so I guess she considered me a contributing member.

I had to admit that she was exceptional. And that I never wanted to play with her again so long as we both should live. But especially never against her.

After she wiped the floor with Germ and his cousin, Betsy suggested going out for a treat. We hit the ice cream place by the freeway, and when the bill came, Jeremy took another step toward making her part of us. Jerk. He explained that it was his turn, and next time, she could pick the outing and carry the bill.

"Leigh's taking us to Chicago for a White Sox game in July," he joked.

"You wish. But I'm thinking a visit to the opera is overdue."

Smiling, I said it was time to switch. Automatically Jeremy and I traded ice creams.

Awkward moment number three hundred twenty-nine of the past several weeks. As usual, Germ to the rescue: "Do you want to try mine? It's awesome. Pass yours to Leigh." He snatched his sundae out of my hand and slid it over to Betsy. Apparently Rat Guy never shared. Okay with me. Who picks peanut-butter ice cream with gummy bears anyway? He claimed it was like a PB&J, but had no reasonable response when I asked about the lemon ones.

Chapter 3

Oh, finally—what a relief. College acceptance arrived, complete with scholarship and housing allowance. This was payoff for years of study winning out over laziness. Mom did the Traditional Dance of Joy (which used to be the Traditional Mason Dance of Joy) and ordered a stunning bakery-made cake sporting the IU logo and covered in red icing that was sure to dye our insides permanently.

In an effort at fairness, she also ordered a green-and-white, tennis-racket-shaped cake for Betsy, even though she had apparently known for months that she had a tennis scholarship to Colorado State. It was a gracious gesture, I'm sure, but come on. This day was not about Betsy. This was my celebration. My achievement. And I'd gotten my scholarship for academics. Who cared if someone could hit a little ball with a racket? I'd used my brains to get into school.

Mom sliced cakes—and everyone got a piece of both—as Paul's hand rested low on her back. I was not getting used to that anytime soon. He passed Betsy her plate and said, "For the Ram," and slid mine to me saying, "For the Hoosier."

"What is a Hoosier, anyway?" Betsy asked.

Mom, Sarah, and Emily all gave me The Look. "Go easy on her, will you?" Mom said.

Rolling my eyes, I shot back, "Well, she asked," before I launched into my dissertation.

"You'll probably get a different answer every time you ask someone that. Most people like the theory that it's a perversion of 'who's here?' following a knock at the door. That's what I learned in fourth-grade Indiana history. A more sophisticated and manly explanation is that it describes a 'husher'—a guy so tough that he could shut up a crowd. Apparently this state's full of those. My personal favorite refers to the cleanup of a bar fight—you know, 'whose ear?' But it was most likely one of those words like 'redneck' that was meant as an insult and then some dumb Indiana boy decided he liked it. Now we are Hoosiers, one and all." I took a bow.

"No further questions, Your Honor." Paul banged the counter with an ice-cream-scoop gavel.

"Leigh knows everything," Sarah offered.

"And she always wants to tell us about it," Emily graciously added.

"What's the good of knowing stuff if you don't get to spread it around?" I asked.

Just between you and me, I admit that *Hoosier* is a dumb word and a bizarre mascot, but I'd rather be a Hoosier than a Ram. That's all I'm saying.

———

Jeremy came to celebrate with me (us) later that evening. We ate more cake (bring it on, baby) and watched a movie:

Hoosiers, natch. He sat between Betsy and me on the couch. I loved being able to forget that she was there for a few minutes. As long as I kept my eyes on the screen, I didn't have to notice her. But if I glanced down to the floor, I could see her ridiculously long legs stretched out next to Jeremy's. Yikes, their feet were reaching the same point. Was she really that tall? I curled my feet under me to sit up higher on the couch.

Paul brought down popcorn later, as if we needed more food (okay, we ate every kernel), and once again Betsy intruded on my notice. Her fingers were so long they spanned the entire bowl. I had to look before I grabbed popcorn so I didn't accidentally touch her. So much for relaxing with a feature film. I was on high alert for at least ninety-five of those one hundred fourteen minutes.

"What? You mean like a date? You're kidding."

"I know, I'm not much of a dater, but I want to give it a shot. You know, test the waters." Jeremy not much of a dater? That was the understatement of the decade. It wasn't hard to imagine why he wanted to discuss this with me: I was his resident expert on what impressed girls. Although, honestly, I was more a theoretical expert than a practical one where dating was concerned. I didn't go out much more than Jeremy did.

"Well, I wanted to talk to you about it first. I want to know what you think."

"Germ, I think it's delightful, and frankly a relief that you still like human females."

"Not about the date. About the girl." He laughed.

I shrugged. "Go for broke. Ask out the whole dance squad, for all I care. As long as it's not Betsy."

Jeremy wasn't laughing anymore. In fact, he looked distinctly uncomfortable.

"That would bother you?" he said.

I forced myself to take him seriously, just in case he wasn't joking. But he had to be joking. Didn't he? "Bother me? Why should it? I was just kidding." And so were you, right? Right? *Right?*

"Good. I'm so glad. Because I want to take her out, but there's no way I would even ask her if you didn't want me to."

If I didn't want him to? What did he think, that I sat home each night hoping that he'd get up the nerve to ask out Betsy? I couldn't fathom a situation where I would Want Him To *anything* with Betsy. I would have actually been thrilled if he'd hated her and I could have had him back to myself. I could let her fend for herself, find her own friends and all that.

As a matter of fact, I hated the idea of Jeremy and Betsy out on a date. I hated the thought of her alone with him. He was *my* friend. But since I didn't have anything like a good reason, I lied. "Sounds like fun."

Betsy actually brought it up too. She asked me if I thought it was okay for her to go out with Germ. I struggled between being glad she'd bothered to ask and annoyed that I had to say it was fine. What else could I say? *No, I'd really rather you stay far, far away from my friends, my family, my house, my city?*

My sarcastic "that's just lovely" clearly hit the intended note, and I felt comforted that she looked hurt. Technically, I'd said yes, so she had no room to complain. But she also had no reason to doubt my feelings. Well, what did she expect? A parade in her honor? Not in this house.

⁓

"Leigh, I just want you to help me make the room look nice. Tell me which fork goes where—like that. You're great at that stuff." He pulled the car into my driveway.

"You've asked her for a breakfast date? I didn't know people did that." As if Jeremy cared what "people" did. Besides, he was playing to his strengths. I had several times fallen victim to Jeremy's astounding waffle-making ability. Any thoughts of moderation or delicate appetites flew right out the back door when these waffles were in the picture.

"First fork you use goes outside. On the left. Then you work your way in. You can handle it."

"Come and show me," Jeremy prodded.

"Just look it up online. You can find a simple graphic to copy directly to your dining room table."

"Come on. Won't you help? I can't do it without you."

"Germ, you're pushing my buttons."

"Well, is it working?" He grinned and squeezed my arm.

"Yeah, okay. I'll help you set up. Come by after dinner."

"I don't want her to know I'm coming, so I'll just knock on the window for you." How many times had that happened in the last few years? He used to get his bike tires stuck in the muddy flowerbed under my window. When it was my window. Looks like nothing that was all mine is all mine anymore.

"You may or may not have been told that Betsy and I are now sharing that room, so you just can't come tapping on the window and hope the right girl answers." I had to stop talking—I could feel that edge coming into my voice.

"Hang on." He said it almost like a question. "You share a room? How did that happen?" Was it possible that we had not discussed this? Well, it wasn't like Jeremy would regularly hang out in my room. Besides, did it change anything to talk it to death? No matter who I may or may not have mentioned our sleeping arrangements to, Betsy and I were still sharing a room, and it looked like we would be doing so until one of us moved out. Or disappeared.

Deep breath. Sarcastic smile. "I know it looks like Buckingham Palace from the outside, but please recall that you have been in this house once or twice. There's not exactly room for two families in here. Some people choose togetherness; some have togetherness thrust upon them. I think it's our parents' idea of bonding. If we see this much of each other, we'll fall logically into complete sisterhood. With any luck it will happen before graduation and the summer holidays."

A year ago, or even a month ago, he would have unquestioningly taken my side, validating my point of view and laughing at the ridiculous idea that close quarters help produce emotional intimacy. I waited for him to pick up on his cue and join in mocking my new family arrangement.

"You know, Leigh, you're not the only one being inconvenienced here. Betsy has to get used to all this too. Consider the small possibility that you are not the easiest person to move in with. And she had to leave her home and her friends and everything. She's starting completely from scratch here. And your mom and Paul have plenty to adjust to just being married. Not to mention your mom's still getting over every-thing with your dad. And the twins have—"

"Thank you, Dr. Bentley. I'll have your check ready on our next visit. I have had enough analyzing for today. I'll wait for you outside at seven." I jumped out of the car and ran up the walkway. What made him think I wanted to look at anyone else's side of this stupid family? I was supposed to be the one he cared about. Since when did my mom come into it? And he was just way too interested in Betsy's feelings. Not good. Let him see and admire her pretty face and get over it. Fast. I was willing to speed that up by being the helpful assistant, Girl Number Two. He could go out with her and find that they had nothing in common. Let's get this date over with and put me back in my Best Friend and Most Important Girl spot.

Late that night as I walked past the twins' room, I pushed open their door and looked in on them. One of the requisite changes in the sleeping arrangements had been to give them my big bed in exchange for their bunk beds. I would rather sleep directly beneath a heavy board that could, at any moment, crush me to flatness than share a bed with Betsy. When my eyes adjusted to the dark room, I found the twins in the mounds of blankets. Could that pile be two smallish chil-dren? There seemed to be twelve elbows there, at least. They looked like kittens, all cuddled up together and wrapped around each other. It was sweet to see them so comfortable and intertwined.

They must have slept like that for months inside Mom. It was an astonishing, spiritual thought. How would it be to love someone like that, just because of how you were made? To actually be the other half of someone? To complement her and have her complement you? Feeling rather small and incomplete, I had just started to back out of the room when Sarah jerked her arm right into Emily's cheekbone and they both mumbled in their sleep. Shifting around, they got contented again. I laughed and blew a kiss. Maybe it wasn't as perfect as it looked.

Chapter 4

Leaning over the counter wiping off peanut-butter sandwich crumbs, I heard the front door open. Betsy came grinning around the corner.

"Hey. How was your date?" I mustered no enthusiasm until the last word. I'll admit, it sounded more like an accusation than an attempt at conversation. But she smiled graciously and told me how great Jeremy's house was (as if I were unaware) and what a fantastic cook he was (thank you for that news item) and that he made the best raspberry-peach smoothie anywhere (my recipe).

I didn't really want to hear any more, so I turned my back to her and rinsed out the cloth in the sink. She apparently missed the body language hint; she wanted to chat.

"He seems like a really neat guy." *Neat?* Oh, brother. Who says that? Was she offering her approval on my choice of friends? Because I certainly did not need it.

"Yep. He's terrific. And he grows on you. After four and a half years, I can hardly get rid of him." My gentle reminder that he was *my* friend was misinterpreted.

"I can't imagine why you'd want to get rid of someone that

great. You're lucky to have a friendship that's lasted so long." She walked over to the sink. "Do you want some help? I can finish up in here for you."

"No, you've had a big day. Go relax. I'll take care of the dishes." I tried to sound sincere, but I think she was learning not to trust any semblance of sincerity in my voice.

She headed out toward the hall but never got past the dining room. She pulled all the chairs away from the table, shook the food from the really crummy ones, and came back in for the broom beside the fridge. As she swept, she said, "Leigh, I can tell you're angry. I thought we got this all straight the other day. I asked you if you minded if I went out with Jeremy, and you said no. I thought that was the end. Now you're acting all grouchy."

"I'm fine. I'm certainly not *grouchy*. I've just got a lot to do, and I don't feel like having a Family Moment with you. That's all. I'm thrilled that you were impressed with Jeremy. You're showing good taste. See you later."

Closing the front door way too hard, I felt a lot better. Making her the bad guy was way easier than being mad at Jeremy and then trying to make up—making up is not my personal forte. I called to the twins to grab their helmets and come for a ride with me. We biked a few blocks to the park and I pushed them on the swings until they got tired of that; then I huddled on a frozen stone bench while they climbed bare trees and made monkey sounds to each other.

In a way it was comforting to see them play together, to watch their bizarre reactions that seemed totally natural to them. Listening to their conversations was like walking in late on the punch line of some joke—I heard words I recognized, but couldn't figure out what they meant. It was like their whole life together was one of those "had to be there" experiences.

Jeremy and I had memories like that, things we never needed to explain. Was he going to want to let Betsy in on them now? Would they even mean anything anymore if he padded them with explanations and descriptions? Could our history expand for another person? Was there room for three? Certainly not. And with no room for an extra, I wasn't about to let all the good things I had going get snatched away from me. I would protect what was mine. But I'd have to be cautious about it.

Being a little jealous of the twins was normal. There was just something so right about how they were two parts of the same whole. Physically, emotionally, they were two of a kind. When I felt left out, that was okay; it was fine for me to admit that I sometimes wished I lived inside that circle. But I felt unwilling to say the same about this new situation with Jeremy and Betsy. For obvious reasons, that was just awkward. I shouldn't want to be inside their new circle—because, well, yuck.

This was not just Jeremy being nice to my stepsister. Jeremy was being way beyond nice. He was nice to me. But he didn't take me on dates. He liked me—loved me, even. But this wasn't about liking me. This was about liking a *girl*. I'd have been Germ's best friend if I'd been a guy. Betsy would not have been his date if she hadn't been a stunning beauty. This was all about Jeremy having me as a friend and deciding that was not enough. He wanted Betsy, too. And *friend* wasn't the word for that.

It was already clear that Betsy wasn't going to push Jeremy

away. She was hooked, I could tell. And unless she developed some unpleasant character traits pretty soon, I couldn't see any reason he wouldn't continue to like her. Just because *I* didn't like her—well, that probably wouldn't make any difference. And if it did make a difference, it would probably make the wrong difference, because Jeremy wasn't the kind of guy to be rude or exclusive. Betsy just might be here to stay, I realized. Which was too bad, because I didn't want to be the one to get squeezed out.

Keeping a balance would be tricky. If I pushed myself in and got too involved at this point, Jeremy wouldn't feel touched that I wanted to be part of what he was doing. It would seem nosy. Or worse, meddling. If he were in any way normal, he would feel challenged, and possibly grossed out. He would feel an ultimatum (her or me), whether I issued one or not. He would not feel flattered by my jealousy. It might actually push him into making a decision I would come to regret— a decision that would bump me right out of the picture. I needed to stay in that picture.

What would I have without him? Not much. My only comfort was that he knew this about me. His place in my life and mine in his—no secrets. We depended on each other. Trusted, counted on, needed, and protected each other. For richer or poorer, in sickness and in health. All that good stuff. That was how we had always been.

Chapter 5

It was a recurring nightmare. I stood in my window trying to catch the scents of an early spring night. The smell of grass growing and buds opening mingled with the lights of passing cars. With my head pressed against the window screen, I could hear the early crickets and assorted bugs and night birds. Then something blocked out the porch light and there he was—a man standing on the porch, his back to me, his elbow resting casually on the door frame. Maybe not quite a man. An almost-man silhouetted in the porch light.

But the voice I heard wasn't his. Much too high and light, with too much sighing, and possibly a giggle. Conspicuously girly—so the guy on the porch wasn't alone. I had that uncomfortable foreboding you get in nightmares when you know someone is going to get hurt, and the distinct impression that it was going to be me. Not every night, but over and over again, it came to haunt me, right before I went to sleep.

The crack of hallway light widened as Betsy opened the bedroom door. I wisely pretended to be asleep, but even if I had been, it wouldn't have lasted. Betsy made more noise getting ready for bed than I had imagined possible for an average-to-tall female.

I understood from her gentle cues that she wanted to talk, but guess what: I didn't. Listening to Betsy's reenactment of being kissed by Jeremy on my front porch was right up there with singing dinosaurs and a bikini wax on my list of things to avoid. Yoga-breathing into the wall, I tried to ignore her and fall asleep.

Drawers opened, rattled, and closed. Clothes swished into the hamper. Desk light clicked on, chair creaked, book pages rustled, pen scratched. Trying not to gag, I pictured her journal entry surrounded by hearts and curly frills. As I attempted to visualize my happy place (far, far away from here), I heard new sounds. Sniffing sounds. Hiccuppy breathing sounds. Fairly unmistakable crying sounds.

Guilt settled in the base of my spine. Though I am capable of being a jerk in multiple ways, I hate to let someone cry alone. It's sort of a policy I have. No one ought to cry alone, even someone who clearly deserves to feel a little distress now and then. I either need to fix it or join in.

Feigning my awakening, I mumbled, "Hey, you're back. Are you okay?"

"Mmm-hmm. I'm fine." Followed by more sniffles. Very convincing.

I slugged out an emotional battle here. Let it go? Be more kind? Believe her? Push for closeness? Remember that it's none of my business? Deciding that "I'm fine" is never the truth, I tried again, "What's the matter? Did you and Jeremy have a fight?"

Wiping her eyes on her pajama sleeves, Betsy returned the

world's most bewildering reply. "He said I was beautiful." More sniffling.

"News flash. You are beautiful. Oh, and by the way, that's a good thing. Most people would like to be told that they're attractive. Really nothing to get worked up about."

She shook her head to dismiss me. "Good night, Leigh." And then, almost too quietly to hear, "You wouldn't understand."

Obviously not.

I flopped over with my face to the wall and willed myself to sleep.

As the dating fiasco marched on, I found myself eager to play with the twins more often. Getting away from Betsy aside, I loved feeling that sweet comfort of adoring little hands. March started waking up the trees and flowers. We played on the swings at the park, we weeded Mom's gardens, we took bike rides on roads where new leaves began to dapple shade on the pavement. We lived like the old days, when we were The Family.

In his defense, Germ tried to give equal time. He attempted visits to me when he knew Betsy was out. He called her when I was supposed to be elsewhere. He hung around our family as if this whole group dynamic was what he really wanted. But there were too many distressing moments of checking our caller ID, finding his number, and wondering if he'd been looking for me or her.

Sarah and Emily skipped into my room and tumbled onto my bed, their favorite storybooks in clutch.

"Whatcha doing? Wanna read with us?" Emily asked.

"I do. Give me a couple minutes. I'm just finishing a fascinating report on cell division." Ah, glorious biology.

"What's that?" Sarah wanted to know.

"Something that happens in your body that makes you grow."

"Does it happen in *your* body?"

"Em, it happens in every body. People, animals, plants, whatever."

"What about Betsy's body?" Sarah chimed in.

"Everyone. Even Mom."

Sarah looked disturbed. "When does it stop? How long will it go on?"

"Forever, kiddo. That's what happens. What's wrong? You look worried."

"I don't want Betsy to have any more salad vision . . . whatever you call it. No more growing. I don't want her to get any taller. She'll grow like Alice in Wonderland and won't fit in our house anymore."

"Maybe it's already happened, and that's why she doesn't fit in our house now." Did I just say that out loud?

Emily waved her copy of *Pigs in My Popcorn* at me. "I'm ready to read to you. Are you done yet?" she prodded.

"Two minutes. Get snuggled, and I'll be right there."

The girls flopped around, propping pillows and squirming into place on my bed as I lay on the floor contemplating biology. Cell division didn't account for the way I was changing and evolving. I was becoming more sarcastic, mean, and spiteful. There was only one way to explain that through biology. Mutation. Betsy was obviously causing me to mutate. Why weren't the twins experiencing the same problem? They didn't seem to be bothered one way or another. Was it just me? Why was I so prone to the mutation vibes Betsy was sending out?

Maybe biology didn't explain it. Maybe I needed physics. Something about magnets, opposition, and polar forces. The twins had a combined force that made them strong and perfect together. Betsy and I clearly had highly opposing forces that, as we drew near each other, shot us apart. A force of nature was working to separate us. Okay, well, we can't fight nature. So be it.

"Okay, girls," I said, pushing my notebook aside. "Where are those piggies in the popcorn I've heard so much about?"

After the girls read me their books, I closed the door and enjoyed a rare minute alone. Knowing that Betsy was out with Jeremy (indefinitely), I had some time to be by myself and to think. I now recognized that I had something great in Jeremy's friendship. But it wasn't just now; I'd always known that. When my dad died, I knew I was lucky to have Jeremy. I didn't take him for granted. I felt like he was my consolation prize from God, and I appreciated that. But what could be my consolation prize if now I lost Germ?

I was so not ready to be replaced, because I had no one else to hold on to. Emily and Sarah had each other. Mom had Paul. And if Betsy had Jeremy, I couldn't even have Betsy. Not that I wanted to. She was, in every way, not my type. But where would I turn if he didn't want me to be his best friend anymore?

Don't get me wrong; it wasn't as if I had no friends. But, you know. The girls were giggly and a little dumb. The boys were one-track-mind types, and I was not on that particular track, if you know what I mean. Jeremy and I just fit together. We knew what was funny and what wasn't. We balanced out. He was smart, I was smart(er). He believed in God, I wanted to believe in God. He made me laugh, I made him laugh. He liked to drive, I would be thrilled to never, ever drive. I was shortish, he was tallish. His parents loved me, my parents loved him. It was a match. A little give, a little take. Having had a friendship that simply worked so well, I was terrified at the thought of a less fabulous replacement.

Chapter 6

"I need to take one giant step away from this whole crazy household." I was pacing a path on the lawn while Germ lay stretched out in the grass. March was working its annual magic, waking up the dullest wintertime place in the world and creating a gorgeous spring. Chirping things were making homes in budding branches. My tirade had been lengthy and predictable—and heavily seasoned with my needs and self-pity.

"I know what you need. A boyfriend." That stopped me cold. I turned around and stared at him, hoping for a punch line. "No, really, Leigh. You need somebody that you can hang out with all the time. Someone who will tell you how great you are and laugh at your pathetic jokes. And I think it's time that you should get kissed. Really kissed. Good and kissed. Trust me," he said with his eyes closed and a disgusting little smirk on his face, "it is such a good idea."

Where had this come from? What was he doing?

My face started to grow hot. "I thought it was your job to be around all the time and laugh with me. I thought you were the one who was supposed to tell me how great I am. But instead, you're always ready to tell me all the things I'm doing wrong." A look of hurt and surprise was growing in Jeremy's eyes.

"Well, Mr. Bentley, it appears that you may not be the man you thought you were. Being a boyfriend *and* a best friend seems a bit much even for a remarkable guy like you. Since you so politely invited me to find myself someone different to share all my free hours with, I will graciously bow out. You are free. Pursue your chosen course. As of this afternoon, I am out of your way."

"What, are you insane? What are you talking about?"

"Go home, Jeremy. Betsy will call you when she gets here, and then you can come back to spend the rest of the day with your new favorite person. I will be very much out of the picture, so the two of you can do whatever it is that I am thrilled not to imagine. I'll see you around." *But only when I can't help it.*

I walked into the house and locked myself in the bathroom. Feeling ridiculous that this was the only place in the house where I knew I could be alone, I slid down the wall and put my head on my knees. Telling yourself you're not going to cry is the surest way to make the tears come, so I composed the Top Ten List of Reasons to Feel Good about the Current Situation. I wrote it on an empty toilet-paper roll I found behind the trash can.

10. I made this happen. I took the action. I sent him away.

9. Who needs a stupid boy for a best friend, anyway?

8. I'm sure I can find a new friend. Maybe even a boyfriend.

7. Can't I?

6. His judgment is clearly impaired (as manifested by his current choice of female companion).

5. If he's out of my hair I have one less person to worry about.

4. Jeremy is an idiot.

3. I get a lot more homework done when he's not around.

2. Did I mention "idiot"?

1. I am so much better off without him.

As I sat there in the bathroom with my knees under my chin I reflected on Reason Number One. Yeah. A lot better off. Who wouldn't rather sit alone on a tile floor, backside falling asleep, talking herself out of self-pity than lay in the grass on a gorgeous sunny day laughing with her best friend? And I confronted the unpleasant truth that I really stink at Top Ten Lists.

I walked outside. He was still there, under the pear tree on his back, looking so comfortable and relaxed he made me crazy. How could he fit perfectly everywhere? Did he even know what it felt like to be out of place? He was Everyman—as much at home on my slowly greening lawn as at a formal dinner party. And then there was me. I would have been ecstatic to feel like I belonged anywhere.

I walked over to him and kicked the bottom of his shoe. "Are you asleep?"

He pushed up onto his elbows. "Just thinking. You want to go for a drive?"

"Will you promise not to shove me out of the speeding car in a rash attempt to be rid of me?"

He smiled. "None of my attempts to be rid of you are rash."

Wind blowing through the windows allowed me to talk from behind my hair. "Germ, I know I'm not going to surprise you here, but I stink at apologies. Having confessed the obvious, I want to say I'm sorry for flying off the handle. I just—I exploded. Thanks for not leaving when I told you to go away."

"Hey, no problem. My mom always told me a girl means exactly the opposite of what she says, anyhow." He grinned at me sideways as he drove toward his house. Eww. He knew how I hated those girls who would say what they thought guys wanted to hear, and pick at a salad when they craved the double bacon cheeseburger.

"Now that I've admitted that I've been acting jealous and stupid, you owe me a confession. It's only fair."

"Leigh, I'm really liking Betsy. She's really great. She's different from other girls."

"Different how?" As if I didn't know. Perfect, flawless, fabulous, whatever. Yuck. Obviously, in every way, different from me.

"She sparkles. She radiates . . . I don't know. Something."

"Cute vibes?" I joked. This was starting to get a little too deep. We were nearing dangerous territory here. Bring it around to her being cute. Always effective. Easy to discuss her perfect figure, her gorgeous brown eyes, her stunning smile. Allow guilt to fester about his shallow obsession.

"Well, you've got eyes, Leigh. You know she's pretty."

We pulled into Jeremy's driveway and walked in the kitchen door. He grabbed two glasses and opened the fridge. He had stopped asking me years ago what I wanted to drink. Sliding a can of lemonade across the island, he poured me a glass of water from the pitcher in the fridge and brought it to the counter. Handing me the water, he poured his lemonade and took a long drink. I could tell he was stalling. I wasn't about to let that happen.

"Okay, listen. If this were about pretty, I'd get it. She's pretty. I can see that. But there are plenty of pretty girls out there and you don't go all shmoozy over them. I know there's something bigger and deeper and more important that you like about her, because I know you and it can't be all about her looks. I hope you'll tell me what it is. I'll try to understand. But you have to help me, because right now I just can't see this— you and her. This is like some bizarre mystery. You and I are so much alike, how can we see the same person so differently? Why is it that you like her so much and I just can't?" I knew I wasn't being fair. It wasn't like I really *couldn't* like her. I just *didn't*. I wasn't willing to try. Because why should I have to try? She wasn't the kind of girl I was interested in being friends with. And I really didn't get why he saw her so differently.

He stared at his fingers as he twisted on his bar stool— 45 degrees to the right, 45 degrees to the left. The fabric of his jeans was wearing thin and there was a paint splatter on his leg. It was yellow paint. Must have been from when he helped his dad paint his mom's sunroom. I couldn't take my eyes off his knees. I sensed that when he found his words, big changes were coming—changes I wasn't ready for. I willed him to forget what we were talking about. *Forget it. Make a joke. Tell me it's none of my business. Say you hear your mother calling. Don't tell me you love her. Don't say it out loud. Don't articulate this feeling I'm seeing in your face that she's superior to every other female you've met.*

Don't say you like her better than me.

He spoke softly. "It's how she makes me feel about *me* that I like. I feel like something important when she talks to me. I want to be smarter, faster, funnier, better-looking, even taller so I will measure up to what she sees me being. At the same time, I know she doesn't care if I ever turn into Superman, because she likes me like this."

Do you ever have those moments when you know beyond a doubt that you've wasted an enormous amount of time being a jerk? I felt my throat closing up and I practically sprinted to the sink to refill my glass.

As I gulped down the water and tried to blink away my tears, Jeremy said, "She makes me feel like you do."

I was stunned. I had no idea how to respond to that. I dumped the rest of my water into the sink and watched it swirl down the drain. Staring at the backsplash, I reviewed the relationships at hand. *He loves her. She likes him. She has every good reason to hate me, but I have no evidence that she has ever hated anyone because she's just too good for that. He depends on me. (Correction—depended on me. Now he has her and possibly no longer needs my friendship.) He likes me, in the world's most platonic sense. And I need him. He anchors me to reality. He holds so much of my history in his hands. He is, as pathetic as it sounds, the man in my life, and he makes me feel worthwhile. What would I do without that?*

Taking a deep breath, I tried to regain control of my emotions. When Jeremy's hand touched my shoulder, I jumped about a foot and a half, and my glass went crashing into the sink. I shouted, "Don't sneak up on me like that! Are you trying to give me a coronary?" I started madly grabbing chunks of broken glass and throwing them into the trash can under the sink.

If Jeremy ever needed living proof that I was just like other girls, he was getting it right now. This display of way too much emotion was sure to scare any guy. He took a step away from me and said, "Don't worry about it, Leigh. I'll clean it up."

The tears wouldn't stay back anymore. I just stood at the sink crying and mumbling, "I'm sorry." I kept fumbling for pieces of the glass, but I couldn't see them through all my tears. I felt a hot sting, and Jeremy must have been watching because he quickly took my wrist in his hand and looked at my bleeding finger. I started to say, "It's fine—don't worry about it," but he looked right at me and I couldn't say any more. Staring at his hand holding my wrist, I let him lead me back to the counter.

He put me back on the stool I'd run away from and sat down beside me. Softly, he blotted the blood off my fingertip with a clean corner of his shirt. Boy Scout training, I guessed. We were in a clean kitchen surrounded by paper towels and cloths, but he used what was right at hand. After wrapping my little cut, he still held my wrist. I stared at his long fingers holding on to me and wished I could make him never let go. Tears were still flowing, but I was holding it together pretty well. No unpleasant noises were escaping me. Reaching now for a paper towel with one hand, Jeremy gently wiped the tears from my cheeks. When he placed the soggy paper towel on the counter, he checked my little wound. The bleeding had stopped, and he very softly kissed the tip of my finger.

"All better," he decided.

"All better," I whispered, and I wasn't lying (too much). Except that I was terrified, because I knew that it was time for me to talk to Betsy. And talking to Betsy about Jeremy scared me almost as much as talking to Jeremy about Betsy. Almost as much as the thought of losing Jeremy to Betsy. Almost.

Chapter 7

"Hey." I poked my head in and saw Betsy at the desk (my desk? our desk?) writing in a notebook. "You busy?"

She shot me the closest thing to a sarcastic glance I'd seen from that face. "A bit."

Super. Exit. I didn't even have to plan my escape strategy. I started backing out of the doorway.

"Leigh, hold on. Sorry. Come back, okay?" No longer cynical, her eyes looked apologetic and hopeful, like a bad puppy that doesn't want to be sent outside. What was that all about? I was the bad puppy around here. Glancing between the taken-apart bunks, I sat down on her bed (mainly because it was made, as opposed to mine) and took a cleansing yoga-breath. Ready? Okay.

"It's not like I mean to be stupid and evil. I don't sit around trying to find ways to mess you up, to hurt our family." I knew the words, or at least the idea, because I'd been working up to this conversation for hours and days and maybe weeks. The words weren't what surprised me. Just that they were coming out of Betsy's mouth.

Taking my stunned silence for disbelief, she continued,

"Leigh, I like Jeremy. A lot. Maybe more than like. He may be the best person I know, I've ever known. But I'm not *doing this* to you. I have no intention of taking away your friend. I didn't move in here with my little spy kit so I could figure out the surest way of making everyone in this house unhappy." I could see tears forming in the corners of her eyes.

Still at a loss, I figured it was my turn. "Uh, see, um . . ." Witty and conversational. Just what I've always considered myself. Time to try a new tack. "Have you ever been, you know, afraid of anything?"

I actually saw the tears spring from her eyes. They jumped, one from either side of her perfect nose, and landed on her cheeks. I'd never seen that happen; I figured it was just an expression hack writers used when they wanted to say *cried a lot*. Then she smiled. You know that scene in the end of *Casablanca* when Ingrid Bergman is wearing that hat and Bogart tips up her chin and she sort of half smiles at him through her tears? Bergman = Betsy. A half-smile and those two tears on her cheeks, and Betsy was suddenly prettier than ever because she was vulnerable. And trusting. She handed me the notebook she'd been writing in. Paper-clipped to the page was a photo of Betsy, but fifteen years older.

"Is this your mom?" She nodded and those two tears slid down her face. I glanced from photo to Betsy, to photo to Betsy. "You're exactly like her!" Here followed an awkward pause, because I'd apparently found the perfectly wrong thing to say. Betsy's movie-star face crumpled into a look of absolute horror. "I—I mean, you look just like her. Your eyes. And, um, your hair and . . . she's really pretty," I finished lamely, not technically sure what I'd done to discompose Betsy like this.

"Here's what I'm afraid of." Betsy tried to take a deep breath, but a sobby sort of snort happened in her throat. Sensing (appropriately, for once) that this was a wrong moment to laugh, I fixed my eyes on her collar and waited to hear what she feared. After a longish silence, I looked to her face, and she was staring at the photo in my hands.

After a day of misjudged conclusions, you'd think I'd smarten up. No such luck. As stupidly as ever, I asked, "You're afraid of your mom?"

Obviously at this moment Betsy realized she was conversing with the village idiot. She gave me a completely level stare that lasted several seconds—until the next little throat-snort caused her to drop her eyes.

I had to strain to hear her words, even though we sat barely a foot apart. "What if I *am* exactly like her?"

I knew very little about Betsy's Mom Situation, and that was fine with me. We didn't need to reveal every detail about ourselves, after all. Mom told me she had run off with some guy, come back, and run off again. That was enough for me. Not that I'm insensitive to other people's tragedies. But more information about something like that could make a girl feel itchy. Yep. I'm definitely allergic to too many details about infidelity.

"What if I turn out like that?" Betsy whispered. "What if I can't commit? Ever? To anyone?"

"I don't mean to sound ignorant, but how could looking like your mother dissolve your commitment ability?"

"You don't get it."

True.

"Can't you see it's because of the way she looked that she did what she did?"

I would have loved to point out that ugly women left their families too, but it didn't feel like quite the right time. But because I couldn't help it, I made a mental list of the ugly home-wreckers I could think of through the following pause. Beginning in Hollywood and moving on down to Indianapolis.

"She was obsessed with being beautiful. She spent more time in the gym and at the spa and in the salon than with us at home. She made herself obvious. Men obviously noticed. Why wouldn't they? She said it felt nice to be seen and appreciated."

Betsy's voice lowered, husky with tears and shame. "Well, I think it's nice to be seen and appreciated too. What if that's what matters most to me? What if the only thing I'm ever good at is being pretty? Is that all I am? Is there nothing else about me that matters?" She looked at me with her broken heart reflected in her eyes, and I felt a tug. It was like when one of the twins got hurt. That urge to hug and apply Band-Aids, you know? I wanted to fix Betsy. I wanted to point out that she was generous and kind and funny (in a gentle, nonthreatening way) and talented and smart and athletic and . . . oh.

If I validated her now, if I highlighted her positives, if I helped her fix this, her only obvious flaw, it would forever remain my fault that I had to live in the same room as the Perfect Girl.

So I shrugged and said, "You'll be fine."

Ha.

The strangest thing happened. Out of nowhere, the day came when I arrived home to an empty house. Not only that, but its emptiness seemed foreign and distasteful. How bizarre. I walked in through the garage and into the kitchen. It was so quiet. Wandering through the hall and past empty bedrooms, I felt uncomfortable inside all that silence. No music was playing. There was no television, no kid noise. The phones weren't ringing. It was creepy, like a ghost town right inside my house. I hopped on my bike and went out to seek company. I found Mom and Paul at the park with the twins. The girls were in the trees, of course. Mom and Paul were trying their hand at tennis with laughable results. I sympathized with their combined lack of coordination and waved as I moved on.

I pedaled over to Jeremy's house and saw him sitting on the porch swing with Betsy. Contemplating a quick escape, I glanced around to see if I'd been noticed. Jeremy was waving at me, and Betsy scooted away from his side a bit. I ditched my bike in the driveway and climbed the porch steps.

"Hey, y'all. What's up?" I asked, hoping not to get too much information in response.

"Choosing classes. I have to decide what to fill my mind with in the fall," Jeremy smiled.

"You changed your mind yet about college? You know you can't really want to go to school so far away. Take the offer from IU and come to Bloomington with me."

"It's not the moon, Leigh. It's just Utah."

"And what can Utah offer you? Cowboys and Mormons."

Smiling and refusing my bait, Jeremy flicked my forehead with his pencil. "Yee-haw and hallelujah, Sister Mason. I happen to love Mormons and cowboys. And skiing, and hiking, and biking, and mountains in general, and inexpensive world-class educations, and . . . stop me if you've heard this before."

I sighed my defeat. "I'm sure it's great, and they'll love you there. I'm just saying a Germ-free environment is not what I've been dreaming of for my college days. And it's not all about me. Who will you hang out with there? Your grandparents? You don't even know anyone else going to school there." Go, me. Points for generosity.

"Allison Hall and Taylor What's-his-name, you know, the white T-shirt kid? They're both going to BYU in the fall too." How in the world would Betsy know that?

"How in the world do you know that?" I had to ask.

Betsy shrugged. "Allison's in my math class. She knows Jeremy and I are . . . friends, and she happened to mention that she'd be at school with him in Utah."

I'd known Allison Hall since the third grade. She clearly knew Jeremy and I were friends, too, and strangely, she'd never happened to mention her collegiate plans to me.

The lightbulb came on. Oh. Gross. She knew Jeremy and I were friends. She also knew Jeremy and Betsy were . . . friends. That meaningful pause, that was the difference. Eww. Word gets around, apparently.

"So what classes are you looking at?" The subject needed an instant change.

"If I pass my AP tests, I'm looking at skipping over half my freshman generals. I can start with the fun stuff. Chemistry, physiology, psychology, like that."

"Boy, you know fun. And I'm thinking food is also fun. Betsy, let's go make the Mormon Scholar some popcorn." I held the screen door open for her. Heading into the Bentleys' kitchen, I snagged a bag of Super Gooey Butter Madness microwave popcorn from the pantry shelf.

"Have you ever looked into one of these bags before it's popped?" Betsy asked.

"That would ruin it. It would make a huge mess in the microwave if it was open, wouldn't it?" Duh.

"I guess you'd have to sacrifice a bag for science. Want to see? You'll never feel the same about eating this popcorn again." Betsy was giggling. "You'll feel strong urges to pat yourself on the back for bravery. I'm telling you, knowledge is power. You, of all people, should realize that."

Eyes shining, Betsy was giddy. Her grin reached all the way to her dancing fingers. "Know where there are some scissors?" She really wanted to decimate this bag. I found scissors, and while I tossed a second bag in to pop, she surgically dissected the waxy paper. Opening the flap with a flourish and an eyebrow wiggle, she uncovered this puddle of nuclear-waste-yellow gelatinous ooze. Popcorn seeds bravely stood their ground in the lake of semiliquid butter substitute.

I had to admit, I was impressed. I'd seen Betsy eat this stuff. Without a second thought, she would toss a handful in her mouth and crunch it between her perfect teeth. And she knew. What it looked like precooked, I mean. "Wow. That's completely frightening. This stuff could light your insides right up."

As if on cue, the microwave beeped. Betsy dumped the popped Super Gooey Butter Madness into a bowl and tossed both bags in the trash. Grabbing the bowl and heading for the porch, she looked at me over her shoulder. "Coming?" she asked.

I shrugged my shoulders and followed her. She tossed a piece of popcorn into the air and caught it in her mouth. "Mmmm, that's good stuff."

Laughing, I got the door for Betsy. Jeremy had moved a chair over facing the swing so he could sit in front of us while he looked over his printout. Betsy and I sat on the swing and threw popcorn at Jeremy. He caught almost every piece in his mouth. Betsy asked me to toss her one. Perfect catch. Another. Perfect. The next one I sent a little to the left, and she snagged it. Great. Another talent. "This I need. I can't believe you. Is there anything you can't do? I couldn't catch a flying piece of popcorn if I was starving to death."

"Sure you could. Here. Try it."

Covering my mouth, I mumbled, "I'm not sure I can eat that anymore. Like, ever again."

"Oh, come on. Open. I'll lob you an easy one," she laughed.

I felt it bounce off my chin. "Leigh, try opening your eyes. It makes it so much easier to see your goal," Betsy said in a third-grade-teacher voice.

With all my efforts focused on keeping both my eyes and mouth open and facing Betsy, I gasped when a piece of popcorn landed directly on my tongue. I nearly aspirated it into my lungs. Coughing, choking, laughing, I held up my hands for her to stop. Betsy cheered, "We did it! Go, team!" and slapped me on the back. I had tears running down my cheeks, and I could hear the swing's chains rattling. Betsy and I sat and laughed while Jeremy calmly went about choosing his premed classes with a not-so-hidden grin on his face.

April arrived and brought my birthday. Eighteen. Wow. I was beginning to feel distinctly adult. Mom and Paul gave me a local area cell phone so I could drive around and feel connected (nice hint, but I don't want to and you can't make me). Betsy bought me a tennis racket, and I laughed. The twins gave me two cans of tennis balls (Emily had opened hers to hear the air escape; Sarah had left that pleasure for me).

I got a ridiculously large check from my Grammy, and I decided (among some extravagant spending and wise savings) to throw myself a canoeing party. Just me and Jeremy . . . and Betsy. Because I had to. Because it would have been too obvious if I had left her out. Because maybe I wanted her to be there. Maybe. Pretty sure that's what I wanted. Weird, but that definitely seemed like what I wanted.

Canoeing was perfect. There were enough clouds to discourage swarms of boaters, but it was warm and breezy and pleasant. A fantastic spring day. Trees were unfolding more and more leaves. Flowers seemed to burst spontaneously into bloom in yards and along roads and in bushes. Rowdy birds accompanied the splashes of our oars. As we paddled along Eagle Creek, Jeremy made comfortable conversation with Betsy about Denver, about Indianapolis, about missing the mountains but (in his opinion) trading up for the trees. Magnificent Jeremy, making small talk with two people he knew very well, just so no one felt slighted.

I was relieved not to be carrying the conversation, and just allowed myself to enjoy the pull of the paddle. Remembering so many canoe trips here with my dad, I reflected how differently things were turning out in my life than I had ever imagined or planned. Some things were even changing in a good way. But it still surprised me how missing my dad could sneak up on me. I could go days without even thinking about him; then that realization would hit me with a slap of guilt. How could I not think about him all the time? I had now officially spent years missing him.

I missed his laugh. He had an out-loud laugh that moved his shoulders. Mom was a *hm-hm* kind of laugher, but Dad would show teeth—and people knew when he was amused. His students at the university loved that. They tried to crack him up during lectures because his laugh was so contagious, and because they could completely derail a history lecture if their jokes got him started. He would so often come home and try to retell a joke he'd heard in class, but he was a terrible joke teller because he would laugh too hard to speak. He could never make it all the way to a punch line. He'd just sag over the counter on his elbows and give up, shoulders shaking and tears starting.

I missed wrestling. He swore kids were made of rubber because of how we'd bounce off the grass when he'd sweep our legs out from under us. The twins were just getting big enough to throw around when he died. A normal, affectionate guy, he was all about hugging after he'd tossed me to the ground. Inside the house, he would tell me we'd better be quiet about it or Mom would bust us for wrestling on the couch. She'd come in and catch us, fake her disapproval, and he'd make me fake a sincere apology. Then he'd stand up to kiss her and toss her to the couch and leap on her in some dramatic wrestling move that would have us all laughing and at least one of us racing to the bathroom.

I missed bike races. We used to race all through the neighborhoods, and we'd sign up together for all the community bike race events. I had a stack of ugly T-shirts (that I wore only to bed) commemorating those races. Somehow I couldn't bear to give them away. Some dads would let their kids win a race as a boost for self-esteem, but his theory was that if he always stayed one bike length ahead of me, I'd never stop pushing for more speed.

For years after I could read, Dad would still read stories out loud to me. He loved historical fiction, but he contended that any story created a history. He read me *The Hobbit* when I was in second grade and lectured (gently, he supposed) about the history of the Shire, dragons, whatever I'd stay to hear. He read to me from his textbooks, from magazines, from whatever he was reading. I loved the sound of his voice.

I missed riding the bus downtown to the university and sneaking into a class. When he'd notice me (which sometimes took a while if he was worked up in a lecture), he'd hum that *Sesame Street* song, "One of these things is not like the others. One of these things just isn't the same . . ." I'd stand up and take a bow, and he'd resume his teaching. After class we'd go to his office and eat toffee almonds until he was ready to head home.

I missed soup. Mom didn't love soup, but Dad had been the Master of the Soup Tureen (which he always called Soup Latrine when Mom was out of earshot—she was not completely amused). He made soup at least once a week all fall and winter for as long as I could remember. There was one with wild rice and celery that I could eat with a fork. And he loved garlic. Garlic made good soup better, he said. He won neighborhood chili cook-offs, and it really seemed like he enjoyed it when neighbors would get sick or have babies because he'd have an excuse to bring soup to other people. Serious comfort food. But after he died, the soup tradition went away too. As I paddled through the murky water near the banks of Eagle Creek Reservoir, I determined to bring back the soup. Spring was a good soup season too, right?

"Betsy, how do you feel about soup?" I asked lazily. Not really thinking about what response I expected, I was caught off guard by her pseudo-intellectual, quasi-British accent.

"I'm in favor of most soups. I have an emotional attachment to one or two varieties, and very seldom have I been offended by a soup. A creamy soup is a nice meal, but a brothy soup is a perfect appetizer. I feel that crackers are optional, and that if sourdough bread is offered, it should be spread only with real butter. No margarine. But with my bread-spread comments I digress. Back to the point. I feel charmed by soup. Delighted. Enchanted, even. And you, Leigh? How do you feel about soup?"

"Wow. That was the greatest ever response to a rhetorical question. I have a feeling you're mocking me, though. I must know: Are you in fact 'enchanted' by soup in general?" I laughed.

"Remarkably so." She smiled and looked to Jeremy. "And you? How do you feel about soup, Jeremy?"

Looking from Betsy to me, to Betsy to me, Jeremy muttered, "I take the Fifth. You're both nuts." Betsy leaned over and splashed a handful of lake water at Jeremy.

"Let's go home and make some soup. I'm not bragging, but I can make a pretty mean bowl. You can come too, Mister, if you can muster the proper excitement," she grinned.

"He'll love it. I guarantee nobody could be served a meal from the Latrine and not enjoy it." Their mingled looks of horror made me laugh out loud.

Chapter 8

My dad's mother lived in Oklahoma. By choice. Dad had been her only child, and her husband had died before I was born. She adored me. She liked the twins, of course; everyone liked the twins. But she had a special place in her enormous heart carved out just for me, and I couldn't imagine anyplace I'd rather be.

Among Grammy's eccentricities, she loved to spring surprise invitations. The week of my birthday, she phoned to say she'd bought tickets for me and Betsy to fly to Oklahoma for spring break. Betsy tried to decline, which I thought was terribly noble of her. She ought to start looking for a summer job. True, but Grammy rarely accepted a *no*. The tickets were ordered, and we would simply break her heart if we didn't come.

As we geared up for the trip, we tried to do a few more Leigh-Betsy-and-Jeremy activities. Germ took us for a Saturday picnic to the zoo. He walked tactfully between us and put his arms around both our shoulders. He joked about our bizarre love triangle and told us if he could always pick two girls to spend the day with, we'd be the girls nine out of ten times.

Somehow Betsy managed to ride shotgun about half the trips these days. It was strange, and a little sweet, to see them holding hands in the front seat. They were significantly less gross than they might have been, and I felt myself loosening up about being the third wheel. Who used to be the second wheel. Jeremy managed to include me by talking to me in the mirror as he drove, which was probably safer than watching Betsy while driving.

When he drove us home, I found myself regularly launching out of the backseat and into the house. At first I thought it was to avoid embarrassing good-bye scenes, but after a few times, I realized that I was stepping aside to give them time alone. And it didn't feel lonely and I wasn't abandoned. Kind of my little sanction on this relationship of theirs.

One night, after just such a quick getaway from Jeremy's car, I watched them out of the living room window. I wasn't being voyeuristic (too much), just curious. He had taken his seat belt off and had his arm casually slung over the back of her seat. They talked for a few minutes, and I found myself wondering what they needed to say after I was gone.

She was laughing at him in her guarded way, eyes down, hand by her face. He reached over to brush the hair off her forehead, and his fingers glided over her cheekbone and down under her chin. He raised her head up gently, leaned forward, and kissed her. I'd never seen them kiss before—they were too kind to go for it in front of me—and I wanted to cry. Not because I was jealous, but because it was just about the prettiest non-film kiss I'd ever seen. Like watching the moon rise red through the trees. Like a new baby sleeping. Like any one of a thousand perfectly natural moments in life that simply seemed right. I wondered if there would ever be a moment like that for me. Not that I was looking too hard, or trying for anything at all. I just wondered, for a minute, what it would feel like to be adored like that. To have someone totally wrapped up in me. To be the most important person in the world, even for a minute.

———

Germ's birthday was the week before we left for Oklahoma. Not that the boating episode wasn't fantastic, but Betsy and I wanted to do something really memorable for him. We were about to leave him all alone for nine long days, after all. So we planned a day trip to the Children's Museum. We told Mom and Paul that we'd give them a Saturday alone and take the twins with us, but we didn't really need them. We would have loved that place even without them. Of all the great places to spend a day indoors, this was way up on the list.

As I paid, I looked over my shoulder and saw Betsy staring up at the polar bear standing on the second balcony. At the same moment that Jeremy went to take her hand, Emily and Sarah each grabbed at her, and Jeremy was tossed. I wondered if he felt it. Did it bother him that someone else was monopolizing the attention of the person he wanted?

According to habit, we ran up the spiral ramp all the way to the top floor. As we rode the antique carousel (after assuring Sarah that her horse would go up and down and Emily that hers would not), Jeremy amused the twins by playing cowboy on his tiger. He sang "Rawhide." I didn't know that song had words—maybe he was making them up. Betsy laughed as hard as the twins, but I rolled my eyes. No use swelling his head too much.

Exhibit after exhibit, floor after floor, the twins showed Betsy their favorite rooms and sights. When we reached the bottom floor, we had to do the Fish Dance. The museum had, among many excellent features, a blue-screen TV setup where kids put on fish costumes to "swim" while watching themselves on a monitor projecting them into an ocean scene. Okay, I'll confess—this amused me as much as it did the twins.

Dressing for the Fish Dance, I caught a glimpse of Jeremy and Betsy in the screen. I had to do a double take because I thought I was looking at strangers. The truth was, I was looking not at two people I knew pretty well, but at a couple. A pair. A set. As I shoved a fidgety Emily into her fins, I watched over her head as Jeremy put crab arms on Betsy. He pulled her hair out from under the costume and kissed her on the cheek. I hated the feeling of jealousy that wrenched at my heart. That whiny, petulant *what about me?* feeling. What did I expect? Did I think he'd come over and kiss my cheek, too? Of course not. But I wanted him to remember somehow that he also cared about me.

Looking away, I managed to wrap Sarah in her fish suit and toss on a mask and snorkel. We danced around and watched ourselves on the screen and looked ridiculous. I avoided Betsy's eyes—I didn't need a glare of triumph from her right now. Not that she would ever shoot me one; she was too generous for that. But still, if we were switched and I had the chance, I'd probably be doing the Victory Dance in her face all day long. Just one more difference between the two of us, the Golden Child and the Black Sheep, the Good Fairy and the Wicked Witch, the Nice Girl and the Evil Stepsister. *Shake it off,* I told myself. I knew what Jeremy would call that, too. *Projecting.* Attributing my feelings to someone else. He'd told me more than once that I was a champion Projector. Yeah, well, if people were smart, they *would* feel like me. So really, I was giving a compliment. Right? Yeah, something like that. *Let it go.*

Winding through the last exhibits, we came into the mummy room. Dark, cool, and just gross enough to be completely fascinating, this was my favorite place. We touched, smelled, poked, organized, researched, and puzzled our way to the Real Live Mummy (Emily's name for the museum's treasure).

"When I die, I want to become a mummy," Sarah sighed over the mummy with a dreamy gaze. This was not an auspicious beginning. I had a feeling I wouldn't like this conversation at all.

"They'll have to pull your brains out through your nose. That's gross," Emily said. "You know you wouldn't like it."

"I'm not going to care, Em. How would I even know? I wouldn't feel anything after I'm dead." How could she say those words like that? So matter of fact. I shivered.

"Well, then, how would you know if we made you a mummy?" Emily shot back.

"Everyone would know I was a mummy. My face would be painted onto the box." Certainly. This was only theoretical, right? I could shake off my discomfort.

Trying to laugh at the twins, I marveled how easily they could talk about this—about their own deaths. They really had no idea what it would do to us, to me, if anything happened to them. Life, death, burial all lumped into a cosmic, distant future to them. It was like a fairy tale. What happens after "happily ever after" is over? Could they know that I worried every day about losing them?

My life felt wrapped tight around these two little girls. I knew I loved them because they were my sisters, but I also liked them. I liked their company. I liked hearing them squeal and sing and giggle and be happy little people. I liked watching them learn things and grow up and be proud of their accomplishments. Mom called it my "mother heart"—a phrase I'm sure I'll understand and appreciate someday. But for now, I squeezed them close to my sides and vowed once again to keep them safe.

"Happy birthday, dear Germy, happy birthday to you . . ." we sang over Ritter's frozen custards. Jeremy beamed. We all dug in to cold, creamy goodness.

"When Betsy and Leigh are gone to Oklahoma, you can still come over and see us," Sarah said through a mouthful of raspberries.

"Thank you, my lady. I would be charmed."

Giggling, Sarah whispered, "He thinks I'm a princess!" She and Emily shared a smug, knowing look.

"What are you going to do with yourself while all your entertainment is away?" Betsy asked.

Jeremy took a huge spoonful of his Heath Bar Glacier and looked thoughtful. "I plan to watch every movie I love that you both hate—cowboys, car chases, ghosts, and terror. I will read car magazines and watch sports highlight shows. I think I'll flex my muscles at myself in the mirror. I'm planning to sit around for a week eating nuclear microwave popcorn and wallowing in my loneliness. It will be pathetic, but hey—I can afford pathetic while I'm alone. I expend a huge amount of energy being charming when I'm with you two. Frankly, I'm exhausted. P.S. Time to switch." Cups of custard moved clockwise one place with military precision. I grudgingly gave up my chocolate-covered banana shake for Emily's Snickers.

"Presents!" Emily called out. I pulled out a backpack filled with Jeremy's birthday gifts. Sarah and Emily had bought him a box of rubber gloves. Betsy and I had taken them to the medical supply store to pick them out. He feigned delight and immediately blew one into a balloon to amuse the girls. "That's for when you're a doctor," Sarah explained. He assured the twins that he loved the gloves.

Mine was next. I gave him an IU sweatshirt, hat, and flag for his dorm room. He laughed and promised to think of me every time he looked at them.

Betsy's gift was a giant container of lemonade powder. And a mug. With her beautiful picture on it. "It's perfect!" he announced. Well, it looked perfect, anyway.

"Time for the traditional Bentley Family Birthday Wishes," he announced. Betsy looked questioningly at me, and I assured her that she wouldn't have to do anything but sit and smile.

"Emily," Jeremy began, "I wish that next year you will be the tallest kid in second grade." Emily laughed—we all knew that would never happen. We didn't do tall in the Mason family.

"Sarah, I wish that you will become the fastest skater and have no more wipeouts." Her eyes lit up as she fingered the scab on her knee.

"Betsy, I wish that you will become a tennis coach this year and teach me to play almost as well as you and then let me beat you in a match, just once. And Leigh, for you I wish you'll meet Prince Charming in Oklahoma. I wish you a spring break fling that will go down in the record books."

I was blushing. Probably at the idea of a redneck romance. But maybe at the idea that Jeremy was suggesting it. Again. Sarah and Emily giggled. Betsy smiled at me as if nothing would please her more than to have any of those impossible wishes come true.

Chapter 9

"My Grammy is possibly the coolest lady you'll ever meet." Betsy nodded. She was flipping through the in-flight magazine as if, by some miracle, there could be something in there to interest her. She'd been fidgety all day, going to the bathroom three times in the airport. "I can't use an airplane toilet. There's not even enough room to turn around in there." I wasn't sure what turning around she thought she'd need to do, but that was certainly her business alone.

Finally it dawned on me that she was nervous. "Is the flight making you jumpy?" I asked. "We've only got a half hour left. The worst part is all over, anyway. Clear skies over Oklahoma City, the captain said. Don't worry about it." She looked surprised. I figured she was still unused to my attempts at kindness, and immediately I felt embarrassed and stupid. I'd promised Mom I would try, but I wasn't very impressed with myself. But she actually reached over and held my hand. "I'm fine with the flight. It's getting off the plane that I'm worried about."

"It's just Oklahoma, not Jupiter. Okay, it is foreign, and if you thought you were about to heighten your cultural awareness, you're out of luck, but there's nothing to stress about. It's not even tornado season. No worries." She was still clutching my arm. Sensing that I had once again missed the boat, I asked, "What do you think is going to go wrong?"

"What if she doesn't want me?"

I actually had to stop and consider: Who was she talking about?

"Grammy? Are you kidding? She invited us, didn't she? Of course she wants you to come."

"I just don't want to bust in there and get in the way."

For a fleeting moment I wondered whether that thought had ever entered her mind when she and Paul had moved into our house. Then I felt completely ungenerous, and again I wanted to make her comfortable. This bizarre sensation of protectiveness surprised me now, and I wondered if, despite all my intentions, I was beginning to think of Betsy as my sister.

Oklahoma can make me dizzy with flatness. Its lack of trees and hills gives me the crazy feeling that I need to manufacture a way to stay attached to earth. All physical features and interesting plant life seem to have been sucked from the state in a series of monstrous tornados, and nobody but me misses them. Neighborhoods look normal enough, but driving down the highways gives me a floaty feeling. The streets, roads, and freeways in Indiana look like landscaped gardens compared to those in Oklahoma. Life somehow seems to carry on normally within this serious want of something to look at and anything to do. But where Oklahoma lacks depth, Grammy has it in spades. I didn't feel it possible to describe Grammy to Betsy, so I didn't really try—but I did give her a heads-up about the food clichés.

"Food clichés? What does that mean?"

"It's probably because she's from Oklahoma City, where there's nothing to do but eat. But she's all about the food metaphors. And everything has a color."

"Everything does have a color," Betsy agreed.

"Not like lizards and sunsets and carpet samples. Like feelings. Fear, nervousness, laughter, and excitement."

A huge grin spread over Betsy's whole face. I suddenly regretted letting her in on this odd piece of Grammy before she saw how fantastic she was—as if I had misrepresented my Grammy to the jury. As Betsy started to laugh, she said, "Getting into bed with cold toes is a grayish-blue feeling. And making a new friend is orange. Light, peachy orange to start, but once you really feel comfortable, it's dark orange like a fire."

I stared. This could not be. Was she going to know my Grammy even better than I did? Would this similar strangeness between them push me to the outside? Would Grammy decide Betsy was more interesting than I was because she could identify the color of her loneliest day? As we began our descent into Oklahoma City, my stomach pitched hard for such a calm flight.

"Hey, baby!" I heard Grammy's theatrical and completely bogus Oklahoma accent as soon as the doors opened to curbside pickup. I ran over and lifted her up in a squeeze. Betsy hung back, but as soon as I let her go, Grammy's arm shot out and wrapped her up. "Why, Miss Elisabeth, aren't you just the most gorgeous thing since burnt sugar on a crème brûlée?" I glanced at Betsy and rolled my eyes. Here we go. Grammy winked at Betsy and stage-whispered, "I just put this accent on for ambience. It makes visitors feel like they're someplace exotic."

"As opposed to reality, which screams all around us that Oklahoma is not exotic at all, but windy and barren, and much too hot," I smiled at Grammy.

She winked at us both. "Well, then, I reckon we'd better get you inside someplace inviting and glamorous before y'all jump right back on that plane and leave me here alone with the wheat fields."

Grammy has a theory about self-esteem and body image. She's convinced that every woman should love at least one part of her body. She has chosen her feet. "Gravity is your friend now, baby, but give it sixty more years and we'll see what's riding where. I chose my feet decades ago, and they have never failed to love me back." Grammy wiggled her perfectly pedicured toes inside her Jimmy Choo sandals. Mom thinks it's slightly scandalous to wear shoes that cost more than her monthly grocery budget, but hey—Grammy feels gorgeous, and I say leave her alone and let her splurge.

"So, Betsy," Grammy spoke into the rearview mirror, "what's your favorite part of you? And no fair picking something internal. I want to be able to see it." I stifled an urge to sing the praises of Betsy's spleen or liver.

"I don't know. I've never really thought about it. Leigh, you go first."

"Ears." No modesty or humility here.

Baffled, Betsy stared at my head. "Your ears? Are you kidding?"

"I adore my ears. Ears are awesome. Did you know they are like fingerprints? The post-revolution Princess Anastasia

Romanoff of Russia was almost identified by her ears. Some girl named Anna had ears that looked just like hers, so they thought they'd found the missing princess in Maryland or something. Except she turned out not to be her, most likely because she was dead along with the rest of the family, which is really too bad, don't you think? And anyway, what's wrong with my ears? You don't think they're fabulous?" I asked, flipping my hair back.

I could practically hear the wheels turning as Betsy digested my Random History Moment and struggled to craft a polite answer. Grammy saved her. "Her ears are just like her father's. He had equally charming ears. And our Leigh is unwilling to appear vain or self-absorbed. So we ignore her obvious unwillingness to play my game and accept her lovely ears." She tucked the hair behind my left ear and sort of petted me.

I tried to imagine Betsy's battle. How to pick the best of so many perfect choices? I couldn't figure her going wrong, but she was evidently taking Grammy's question seriously enough to tick off all her lovely parts and choose the best one: Teeth? Hair? Smile? Jawbone? Eyelashes? Clavicles? Piano fingers? Thighs? Shoot, except for my ears I'd have been willing to trade anything straight across.

"Okay, I have one. I love my triceps."

"Ooooh, great choice. Why?" Grammy prodded.

"Well, it's like you said. Gravity is going to catch me, but until that day I will move my arms with no jiggle and perfect my backhand stroke to postpone the inevitable."

I laughed with Grammy and Betsy, but wondered for just a second if I could possibly have been mistaken, because it seemed to me that Betsy was looking pretty hard to find something about herself to love.

As we drove down the freeway, Grammy announced that she and Betsy were going to have to do some girl bonding. I was being dismissed. She had already arranged for me to have "an outing" with her neighbor Trevor. She assured me he was cute. I believed her. Grammy had excellent taste. Deciding to tuck that information away for later, I determined not to worry about it. What was the worst that could happen, after all? He could be a thirty-five-year-old ex con on parole after a stint in jail for being a stalker. At least he was cute.

After a Jamba Juice smoothie, Grammy treated us to pedicures at her salon. All the women working there knew her by name. She pulled up a chair and watched them working on our toes.

"Pick my color for me, Grammy."

I saw her eyeing me, as if trying to read my thoughts. But I knew she was just determining my emotional color. "Bright blue. Electric blue like a miracle. That's what you need. Something shocking, but pleasant. You know, Trevor has a bright blue feeling about him." I could tell this was a comment that I was allowed to ignore. I could wait to respond until I'd actually met him.

I shrugged at the cute college girl buffing my feet. "The queen has spoken. Bright blue it is." I smiled. Maybe a bright blue miracle was, just like Grammy said, exactly what I needed.

Bless Grammy's heart, she did her best to entertain us. We traversed Oklahoma City's exciting tourist destinations. Both of them. Our visit to the Murrah Federal Building bomb site was tender in dozens of ways, but none more than remembering my first visit there. The year I was six, we visited Grammy for Christmas. The bomb site was a gaping, ragged hole in the middle of downtown. My heart was jumpy—I was sure that someone would come and hurt us while we stood there. Dad knelt down in the dirt and pulled me onto his knee, patting my hair and telling me the story of the disaster. I clearly remembered and understood, even at six, the moral of his story.

"Sometimes terrible things happen. Sometimes they happen because someone makes a choice that affects lots of people. Sometimes awful stuff just happens because things go wrong. People die, and that always hurts our hearts. But there's always something to learn from a tragedy. Do you know what I've learned from this one?"

I shook my pigtails against his shirt.

"I've learned to hold my girl closer, for just a little longer each day. Do you understand? We can fill our hearts with happy memories and hold on to those memories forever."

As I stared into the reflecting pool by Grammy and Betsy, I let myself cry for a minute. I wasn't the only one in tears watching the sunlight glint off empty chairs in this beautiful park, but my tears had very little to do with a bomb.

The next day we experienced Cowboy Culture. Some people may consider that an oxymoron, but those people are, as Grammy so graciously put it, "bozos." Betsy was feeling at home with the whole cowboy thing; apparently hats and horses are big in Denver too. The Cowboy Hall of Fame sits on what passes for a hill just outside the city. After a quick run-through, Betsy and I sat on the grass outside overlooking a movie theater parking lot and nibbling excellent sandwiches and pondering the mysteries of our universe (the one that revolved around us).

"Do you ever wonder if we would have been friends if there was no my-dad-and-your-mom? If we had just met at school, if my dad and I had just moved to Indiana on a whim, would you and I have been able to meet and like each other without all the family issues and emotional junk we have to deal with?" Betsy picked at her lunch. I leaned back on my elbow and let her ramble.

"Other friendships seem so easy—probably because they have a healthy distance going on," she went on. "Something about sharing not only a house but also a shower puts an extra pinch on a relationship. I think we could have been pretty great friends if we'd had a little more space. Maybe even different bedrooms? But you can't have it all, right? At least not all at once.

"You're so much the kind of person I would have looked for to be my friend. You make me laugh and tell great stories. You know the strangest things, and your brain is a warehouse for useless information. Facts come flying out of you like tennis balls out of a serving machine. I never know which direction they'll fly. You know a little about everything and your conversations are hilarious. That's what I love most about you."

Had she just said *love?* Sitting here outside the Cowboy Hall of Fame eating a tuna wrap with lettuce and tomatoes, Betsy had just become a champion of bravery and valor, willing to be the first to leap toward emotional openness. She'd confessed to feeling something huge when she had no way to know how I would respond.

I'd never heard her talk *love* before. I wondered briefly if she'd told Jeremy what she loved most about him. And what that would be. Would she choose the same things I would choose?

But *love* is too ambiguous. The things I loved about Jeremy had nothing to do with a boyfriend, so she must have had a whole different set of things to choose from. Because I loved his floppy hair. I loved his laugh that sometimes still cracked his voice. I loved his ridiculous sense of fashion. I loved his willingness to say what he felt. I loved how he met my eye when he gave a compliment, waiting to see me believe him. I loved his brain—that bizarre way he made connections. I loved his comfort, how he belonged everywhere. I loved his gentleness. Couldn't someone please think of different words to describe the different relationships? I mean, I love caramel popcorn and my bike, but that's just not the same. Neither is the Jeremy-Betsy thing. Or the Betsy-Paul thing, or the me-Sarah-Emily thing. I was starting to get brain overload. I still hadn't responded to her comment—the one that added up to a confession. She deserved a response, didn't she? Were there things I loved about Betsy? Loved enough to admit, to put out into the open? And were those things (even things I *liked* about her) enough to overcome the inconveniences of The Family, and especially of the Jeremy situation?

"Who knows?" I shrugged.

I could think of nothing else to say, so I wadded up my garbage and threw it at her shoe with a grin. She would just have to learn to read my mind—I'd been told that was not the most difficult thing in the world. Thinking it over, I wondered if our challenge did in fact come from living in the same house. Wasn't it more about the whole Jeremy situation, like I'd always thought? Okay, in fairness, probably not. If she were not a member of my household and was Jeremy's girlfriend, I would most likely be there to cheer her on. I could support a girlfriend, probably. And she was good for Jeremy. She was sweet like him, talented like him, musical like him, athletic like him. Maybe she was wound up a little tight sometimes, but she was undeniably a nice girl.

"Let's go find Grammy. She's sniffing around inside hoping to catch a glimpse of Tom Selleck."

Her blank stare begged more information.

"He's a big donor here. He loves this place."

"Who?"

"Tom Selleck." I said it slowly.

"Who is that?"

"Don't you dare let her hear you say that!" I laughed, and we ran inside the museum.

Chapter 10

"Trevor's here, Leigh," Grammy sang.

I snatched a look at myself in the mirror and decided that this was going to have to do. I was wearing capris and a T-shirt and my hair was in a ponytail. I casually hoped that he wasn't too formal a guy. Checking one last time for bits in my teeth, I headed out into the hall.

Grammy had promised that Trevor was cute. Trevor was not cute. *Cute* is for guys who are funny but not too bright. *Cute* is for guys who are decent-looking but not in shape. *Cute* is for anything beginning with "he's a nice guy, but . . ." and Trevor was not cute. Trevor was *hot*. Ridiculously handsome. Black curls hung down over his forehead. I had the bizarre first thought that I wanted to pull on one of those curls to see how long his hair would be if it were straight. (I restrained myself.) He had a wide Polynesian nose and perfectly straight, blistering-white teeth. He had on a plain T-shirt, which didn't totally hide his muscle definition, and cargo shorts. Oh, yeah. Soccer legs. Very defined calves. I was so surprised and pleased I felt myself blush.

"Hi, Leigh," he said. "Your grandma has told me all about you. Thanks for coming out with me."

"Really, it's my pleasure," I smiled at him and turned to Grammy, letting my eyes go wide. Mouthing *Holy Cow*, I smiled, then turned back to him.

"You ready?" I was still blushing. Maybe it would make me look tan.

His car was parked on the street between Grammy's house and his. "Are you a good golfer?" he asked.

"Not remotely. I can sort of mini-golf if the wind is with me, though," I said.

We drove to the games center and he handed me a bright blue putter and ball.

"Thanks for getting me a matched set. Now I won't forget which is mine and accidentally get a hole-in-one with yours," I teased. His golf ball was pink. I thought the girl behind the counter took longer to ring him up than necessary, probably because she was a shameless flirt.

"I'd love to ask you all kinds of small-talk questions, but I'm afraid I wouldn't sound very sincere. Your grandma really has told me everything about you."

"Like what?" I wondered. What was there to tell, really?

"She told me you're a biker. I kind of hoped that meant you wore black leather with a bandanna over your hair, but I'm trying to mask my disappointment. How am I doing?" he asked with a totally fake smile. I laughed.

"She told me when you were small you always used orange-scented shampoo, and every time she squeezes oranges she thinks of you."

Wow. That was really sweet. I had totally forgotten about that shampoo thing.

"She mentioned that you're some kind of genius. Okay, actually she told me you're top of your class, and I promised her that I wouldn't be intimidated by a bright girl. She said you were cute. That's not the word I would have used."

Okay, what was I supposed to say to that? Thank you? I agree? No, you're right, I'm not very cute? With his back to me, he lined up a shot and putted the pink ball into a crocodile's mouth. I had a few seconds to compose my face, to move from unpleasant surprise to politeness.

"Is this game going to be some digestive system anatomy lesson? Where exactly is your pretty little golf ball going to come out?" I asked, changing the subject.

As it turned out, the cup was down a ramp in a nest of crocodile eggs that were losing their painted finish. The overall impression was that this crocodile was probably not the best mother in the animal kingdom. A little neglect, maybe some reckless stomping—either way, you kind of feared for the babies.

I lined up my bright blue golf ball and took my shot. Apparently the wind was not with me. I missed the huge gaping mouth completely. It took me four more shots to get around the beast, down the ramp, and into the cup. Trevor was laughing at me.

"I concede defeat. Want to keep playing, or am I humiliating you?" I asked.

"Are you kidding? I feel like a pro now. We keep going. And we're keeping score."

Trevor lined up for the next hole (after asking me if I

wanted to go first) and shot straight through an invisible alley between nine turtles. When I took the shot, my ball went pinging around from turtle to turtle. At the very same moment, Trevor and I made a pinball machine noise. We both burst out laughing. The ball bounced and rolled and bounced and finally ran out of momentum somewhere between turtles seven and eight.

As I brought the putter back and took my swing, I was horrified to see that I chipped what would have been a nose off the concrete turtle, if concrete turtles had noses. The little chunk of painted cement went flying directly into the cup. Hand over my mouth, I turned, wide-eyed, to Trevor. He was not laughing. I felt like such a clumsy idiot. Very calmly Trevor picked up my ball and patted the now-deformed face peeking out from a purple shell. He walked to the cup, retrieved the cement chip, and dropped my ball in. Walking back to me with a very serious look on his face, he pulled my hand away from my mouth.

"You have to keep this forever," he said, placing the concrete chunk in my hand, "because this represents the greatest series of shots in Oklahoma mini-golf history. Let us make it official," he added, reaching for his phone. Not until he snapped a picture of me did I realize he was teasing.

"I thought you were mad," I said. "I thought maybe your family owned this place and you were personally responsible for seeing that all the fake animals have all their parts and I was causing extra work for you and you were going to take me back to Grammy's right now and never want to see me again because I'm some psychotic turtle defiler."

Now he was laughing. He had such beautiful teeth.

"You have beautiful teeth." I actually said that out loud. But at least it was true.

"Thanks. My uncle's an orthodontist. I'm some of his best work."

Okay, he'd sort of brought up his family, so I could ask, "Are you Hawaiian? Sorry if that was a dumb question, but I've been to Oklahoma City a few times, and I can't imagine leaving Hawaii to move here."

"Have you ever been to Hawaii?"

"Okay, no. Not exactly. But I've seen pictures. And, to be honest, I can't imagine leaving most places to move here."

"I've never been to Hawaii either. My mom is Tongan. My dad's from here, and they met at college in Utah."

"My best friend is going to college in Utah in the fall," I interrupted.

"Really? Me, too. Where's she going?"

"Who?" I asked, confused.

"Your friend. The one going to college in the fall. The one you just brought up."

I obviously sounded like a total fool. Good thing Grammy told him I was smart, because he would never have guessed that on his own.

"He. My friend is a *he*. He's going to BYU. It's a school for Mormons."

"You know, I've heard of it? I've even heard they let other kinds of people in there. That's where I'm going too."

"Does my Grammy know that?" I wondered if this was why she had arranged this date. So I'd know someone else who would be up in the mountains with Jeremy. Or maybe just because she knew Trevor was hot. Either way, it was kind of her.

"Probably. My mom tells everyone I'm going. She's a big fan. She hangs a huge blue flag from our front window whenever there's a football game. She's crazy—in a good way."

"What's a good way to be crazy?"

Placing his pink ball on the tee mat for the next hole, Trevor said, "She's in love with the whole world. She's a big hugger. And an excellent cook. When my friends from school come over, they get a hug and a plate of food. The grill is on just about all day, every day. She loves to sing, especially really tacky love songs. But she has a really deep voice, so it's good-crazy to hear these soft, sweet lyrics coming out like a bass rumble. She's awesome."

I wondered if I should talk about my mom. Somehow I didn't want to, because that would lead into talking about my dad, and about Paul, and about Betsy, and probably about Jeremy, and tonight I just didn't want to go there. It felt so free and breezy to just be Leigh. Not to be tied up inside a huge family disaster or any type of triangle. Besides, if I kept Trevor talking, maybe he wouldn't notice my dismal golfing ability.

We quit golfing after nine holes, when my score reached my mom's age (and she's already seen the happy side of forty). My favorite was the giant mechanical tarantula whose leg joints moved so it went up and down over the hole. Trevor missed that one—he said I was distracting him. All I was doing was humming (way too loud) "Itsy, Bitsy Spider" and making creepy spider legs with my fingers. Was it my fault if he felt distracted? Well, I really hoped so.

After we turned in our clubs, Trevor asked if I was hungry.

"Here's something I guess my Grammy didn't tell you. Not only am I always hungry, I can eat most people I know under the table."

"Dinner, or dessert?"

"Both," I smiled.

"Which do you want first?"

"Did you know that my Grammy regularly orders dessert first at restaurants? Because it's already made, and they can bring it right out to her. She has patience for a lot of things, but not for food. She's got to have it when she's got to have it."

Trevor loved that idea. We drove to what he assured me was a very authentic Mexican restaurant. The hostess said something to Trevor in Spanish and he answered her with what even I could tell was a pretty bad accent.

"Where did you learn your awesome Spanish?"

"Why? Do you speak Spanish?" he asked.

"Nope. I can count to ten because I watched public television as a kid. I take French and sign language at school. Did you pick up that excellent accent in school?" He could tell I was teasing.

"The funny thing about being, um, a Brown Guy around here is that everyone assumes you've come up from Mexico. For years, I'd be riding my bike or walking through a store or standing around talking with friends, and strangers would come up to me and ask me things in Spanish. I got so embarrassed not being able to understand, I decided I needed to learn it just to protect myself from humiliation. So now I know that they were usually asking for directions and stuff, and it's easier not to feel intimidated when a cute little white-haired old lady tries to pick me up at the library or something."

"Does that happen to you a lot?"

"Oh, I love the library. It's my best place to get picked up by sweet grandmas asking for directions in Spanish."

Chips and salsa were on the table, so we didn't have to order dessert first. I dug in to the salsa and I'm pretty sure I started breathing fire with the first bite.

"Do you like it?" Trevor asked.

"Mmm. Hahhh. Wow. Give me a sec," I gasped. This was not like the Mexican food in Indianapolis. I gulped my whole glass of water and wiped my streaming eyes.

"Maybe I should have warned you, they don't skimp on the heat here. You all right?"

"I'm good. This is great. But I can no longer feel my face. Is it still there?"

Trevor laughed, "Try the guacamole. It's pretty tame."

Touching the corner of a chip into the creamy dip, I explained that in Indiana, what our food lacked in spiciness we made up for in volume. And that most good things were made better with a great deal of gravy.

Our waiter made his way through the brightly draped, candlelit tables toward us. "Do you know what you want to eat?" Trevor asked me. I looked at him in panic.

"Could you order for me? Something gentle?"

"Sorry, Toto. You're not in Kansas anymore, and I'm not getting you anything swimming in gravy. How do you feel about cheese?"

"I'm totally into it. Bring on the cheese. Just order me something that won't set my throat on fire, okay?"

"No problem." He ordered for us and asked the waiter to bring some more water. I knew Trevor was laughing at me, but

I didn't really care. I could think of plenty of places less pleasant than this. And having a great-looking guy smiling at me across a small table was perfectly okay.

"So this friend of yours, the one who's not a girl. How did that happen?"

"I don't know. Nothing really happened, we just met at school a few years ago and got along great and liked each other's company. Now we see each other all the time and he loves my family and I love his family and we're just best friends. He's the one I always go to whenever I want to talk, and we have fun together. You know, like friends."

"Is he good-looking?"

"Sure. He always needs a haircut, though."

"Have you ever kissed him?"

None of your business. "Well, yes, but not like you're thinking. Kind of like you'd kiss your brother."

"I'd never, ever kiss my brother. He would flatten me in a second. We're huggers at my house, but not kissers," he grinned. "Have you ever wanted to kiss him? You know, really?"

This was tricky. It had certainly crossed my mind, but the urge was never stronger than the certainty that it would change how things were between us, so it had never really been worth thinking about too much. I shrugged.

"Has he ever wanted to kiss you?"

"Why are we still having this conversation?"

"Well, see, I'm trying to figure this out. I know this girl, and I just met her, and she's great, and she's beautiful, and I've known her for about an hour and a half and I have not stopped thinking about how I'd like to kiss her since I watched her thrash a turtle with a golf putter. So how could a normal, smart guy who sees you every day and knows you so well and has every chance in the world to be close to you just never make a move?"

My ears were on fire again, but not from the salsa. Who talks like that? And what was I supposed to say? I twisted my napkin, realized that I was fidgeting, and set it down.

"I guess he doesn't see me that way. You know, I'm not . . . well, he's not—he likes, um . . . see, it's . . ." I had no idea how to finish the thought. I'm not Jeremy's type? We are the perfect example of platonic love? Jeremy's style of being close to me tends more toward arm wrestling? There's this other girl that I really don't want to talk about? "I didn't exactly *thrash* that turtle." He laughed, but there was a softness in his voice now.

So this is what it feels like to move to the next level. I'm pretty sure I'll like it as soon as I can make myself believe that this is all real. That he's really here, really talking to me, really interested.

I looked at his face and saw him smiling at me and thought *I will get good and kissed tonight.* That was not a thought that crossed my mind very often. Okay, ever. Could I do this? Could I just go ahead and let myself be the kind of girl who gets kissed by extremely hot guys? Or even once, by one guy— a guy I may very well never see again after this week? On a first date? Jeremy would be scandalized. Why did that thought make this so much more interesting? Oh, why not?

Dinner was delicious, but strangely, I was not very hungry. Trevor laughed at me as I picked at my enchilada. "I thought you were a big eater. I have to say, I'm not that impressed," he said.

Shrugging my shoulders, I said, "I guess I'm not as hungry as I thought." Looking at my plate, I smiled. I was definitely full of something—a weird and uncomfortable and exciting something.

"Want to go for a walk?" he asked.

"That would be great."

After he paid the check and I pocketed the mints from the table, we walked outside. He held the door for me, and as he came around beside me, his fingers brushed mine. I felt a shock move from my fingertips to my shoulder and down into my stomach. Wow. He put his hand on the back of my arm and lightly ran his fingers down to my hand. It fit perfectly inside his as we walked a few blocks to a park. He looked down at me, smiled, and gently squeezed my hand. Was this really happening? Was I about to have a spring break fling? I squeezed back.

I simply could not explain what happened after that. He pushed me on the swings. We went down three different slides, like eleven times each. He did chin-ups on the monkey bars and I watched. Specifically, I watched his arms. I'm not actually sure I could describe those amazing arms. We talked, we laughed, we had a great time. Then we walked back to the car and he drove home.

If you're wondering where the kissing fit in, so was I. The dark and deserted playground seemed like a pretty fine opportunity to me, but no such luck. Walking back to the car might have been a little more awkward, but still acceptable. There was a lot of laughing, plenty of flirting, even a little more hand holding, but a total lack of kissing.

Parking the car between his home and Grammy's, Trevor

immediately turned off the engine and jumped out. He walked me up to the door at Grammy's house and gave me a hug. This word *hug* really doesn't do it justice, though. He wrapped his arms (those arms!) around my waist and halfway back again. My face was against his chest and I could feel his pulse. Resting his head on mine, he breathed into my hair. My arms were around his neck and I wasn't about to let go first.

"I'm so glad you came out with me. You're awesome. I mean, at golf. You know."

I laughed. Arms still around his neck, I looked up at him. We stared at each other for about seven hours (more or less) and he smiled and I was dazzled. No one flickered a porch light. No one dropped a glass. No car alarms went off. Nothing really occurred to prevent the kiss; it just didn't happen. And I was sorry.

Chapter 11

"G ood morning, Sleeping Beauty," Grammy said from the stove where she was flipping pancakes. "Look who's here doing my yard."

I pulled back the curtain and saw Trevor's back as he pushed a mower across the grass. Betsy was folded into a kitchen chair, arms wrapped around her legs and chin on her knees, staring out the bay window.

"Grammy," she said, "can you and Leigh have some bonding time tonight? I have this great idea—"

I interrupted. "I guess not. Certainly not. Absolutely not. You're not even allowed to meet him. If you must leave the house when he's looking, you have to wear a trench coat and glasses. Maybe a really big hat. Grammy, do you have a costume supply place around here? We could rent her a fat-suit."

We laughed at that image as we stared out the window at Trevor's retreating back. When he turned the mower around, we all dove for cover.

"Do you think we should eat on the floor?" Grammy asked.

"Yes," Betsy and I said together.

We had a kitchen picnic of pancakes and juice on the floor

next to Grammy's table. If for any reason Trevor had looked in the window, he would have seen three heads behind the table—all of Betsy's, half of mine, and the top of Grammy's hair. He didn't look. We kept watch.

"So, apart from the obvious, what's he like?" Betsy wanted to know.

"Which obvious? The lawn-mowing chivalry?" I was playing dumb.

"That's not chivalry, baby," Grammy corrected. "He's making big bucks keeping my yard. Saturdays he mows, Wednesdays he weeds. I think I bankrolled last night's date. About which I have heard nothing yet, darling. Time to dish." Grammy tapped my plate with her fork.

"We played mini golf and had dinner."

Betsy looked offended. "You can't be serious."

"Which part?" I asked. Did she have something against golf? I was sure she approved of dinner.

"That is not how to dish a date. You must not, under any circumstances, be evasive. You tell all, and you tell it now," Betsy commanded.

I laughed and started to tell about last night. We all let our pancakes get cold as I described whacking the turtle's nose off, gulping salsa that made me want to cry, and swinging at the park.

"He asked about Jeremy. It was funny, like he wondered if Jeremy was . . . competition."

Betsy arched her eyebrows. "Isn't he?" she asked.

"No," I answered too fast. Why would she ask that? She, of all people, should have known where things stood.

"Hmm. Okay." She picked at her pancake. Glancing back

at me, she could tell I was waiting for her to elaborate. "If I were an outside observer, I would have to say that Jeremy is huge competition for anyone who wants time with you. You're with him all the time, and when you're not together, you're on the phone. Jeremy is your ideal guy. Nobody will ever measure up to him. Let me restate that. There has never been—before yesterday—anyone in the world you found as interesting as Jeremy. He's like Yang to your Yin or something like that. Is that right? I forget which one is supposed to be female. But you know what I mean. Jeremy would definitely seem to stand between you and another guy, just because of who he is. Because of who you are."

Translation: I stood between Jeremy and his girlfriend. But she said it so openly, so sincerely, and without any complaint or whining. As if Jeremy was the prize, and I was part of the package. And she seemed okay with that.

Shaking off any gravity from the conversation, Betsy asked, "So did you find an excuse to touch that amazing hair?"

⁓

Stirring a straw through my second smoothie of the week, I snatched a moment of alone time with Grammy while Betsy excused herself to the ladies' room. It had been a good day at the zoo, and we were all having fun together. We'd seen the gorillas and the dolphin show and eaten plenty of popcorn. But I was feeling low. I had a weird guilt about starting to like Betsy too much. I think I needed to keep things in order. First came Mom and the twins, then Dad, even in memory, then Jeremy. Then Grammy, then my guidance counselor and possibly Trevor, and then the Burkes. Okay, maybe not the counselor, but I had to keep things straight. My loyalties were important to me. No one should wonder where anyone fit.

"Betsy is a sweetie. It seems like things are progressing between you girls. You're starting to connect, aren't you?" Grammy practically had to lower her head to the table to meet my downturned eyes.

"I don't know. Sometimes I feel like we're doing great, but then logic comes in and tells me that we have nothing in common. We're really different, and don't we need to be alike to get along? You and I are practically the same, and we're best friends. But I'm not like her. She's so perfect. She's so . . . sincere. I'm just not the kind of person who can pull off *sincere.* At least not on a regular basis."

"Birds of a feather flock together, and they'll likely peck all the poppy seeds off your bagel. Having things in common is not all it's cracked up to be. And anyway, the two of you have parents, siblings, an address, and Jeremy in common. That sounds like a whole lot of something to me." Grammy inspected her cuticles quietly, waiting for me to come around.

"Grammy, I think she and I are too different to magically become best friends all of a sudden. Besides, I have a best friend, and I don't think I need another one."

As I glanced over to see if Betsy was returning from the restroom, I caught Grammy's disappointed look. If I'd been determined to let down all the people I loved, I wouldn't have had to work much harder. I whispered, "Sorry, Grammy." Raising her eyebrows, she shrugged as if to ask what I was sorry about.

"I don't want you to be angry with me, but I can't be someone I'm not."

"Sweet pea, nobody is asking you to change anything. You are just right. And you don't need a friend who's a copy of you. Just think, you might be able to pinpoint all her flaws. And possibly she'd find yours—if you developed any, of course. A friend who is exactly like you is not what you should be aiming for. Last time I checked, Jeremy was not quite exactly like you. There are one or two differences anyone is bound to notice. You don't need someone just like you; you just need to be facing the same direction. Maybe you could just unlock one of those rooms in your heart and let some of our new family in."

Our new family? How were the Burkes possibly hers? Paul was usurping the rightful place of her son. I was only her family because she was my dad's mother. How did that include Betsy at all? Waves of heat poured off my forehead and out of my ears and eyes. I felt my smoothie melting in the jealous confusion. Betsy, who had returned while I was stewing, pulled out her chair and started on her drink.

"You know what I've been pondering, girls?" Grammy began. I felt a Dad-like lecture coming on. Without waiting for either of us to take the bait, she rushed ahead. "Choices. We all chose different smoothies today. They're all good, and even though we each picked something different, we will each be happy with our choice. And I'm glad that you made choices that make you happy. It would be a disappointing trip if you chose a smoothie that didn't agree with you. Such is life." Cue the point. Meaningful smiles to Betsy and me.

"We make our decisions and deal with them, and if our

choices make us happy, we can all be happy for each other. But here's the thing—we all decided to come here together. Our smoothie experiment would have been much less pleasant if Betsy went to a steak place and Leigh needed sushi. I would have been here alone with my drink, and you would have each eaten alone. And paid your own checks.

"It's kind of like that in a family, isn't it?" Grammy glanced from Betsy's eyes to mine as though this had just come to her (and not been percolating for months). "You make the decision to be a family. You head for the same restaurant. Once you're all around the table, everyone can choose what sounds delicious. But the point is, you stay in your seats. You choose to enjoy your meal, even if there are too many croutons in the salad. It's okay to leave some things on your plate. You're not required to love every little detail. And if your food is great, you might just offer a bite to the person sitting beside you."

"And," Betsy joined in with a grin, "halfway through dessert, you switch plates. Right, Leigh?"

"Mmm-hmm." I knew she was trying to make me seem like the good guy, which obviously made me feel like an idiot. I may have been willing to switch desserts, but I wasn't winning any Peace Prizes for ignoring the extra croutons on my salad, if you know what I mean. In Grammy's metaphor, I was building a tower out of the things I didn't care for, and then hiding behind it.

Did Grammy have it right? Was this all a matter of choosing to accept our arrangements? Could I be happy to ignore Betsy's annoying perfection and just enjoy the ride? And for whose sake? For Mom, could I set aside my jealousy? For the twins, could I share my place as Big Sister Idol? For Grammy, could I smooth out the bumps in the path that led to the Burke family? For Jeremy, could I remain the friend-who-is-a-girl and welcome in an actual girlfriend? Not sure, I did what I knew I could do.

"Time to switch," I said, passing my smoothie to Betsy.

———

"I'm not telling. Just get dressed in your finest. No more questions. We're leaving in fifteen minutes. Now go." Grammy was turning into a bossy lady.

"I wonder what this is about," Betsy said.

"There's no way to know. Grammy loves her surprises. We could be going to Texas." Noting Betsy's look of horror, I added, "But probably not. She wouldn't make us get dressed up for that. Let's just enjoy the ride and let her have her secret."

A few minutes later, I heard a knock on the front door as I finished doing my hair. Betsy and I walked down the hall to find Trevor standing in the doorway. He was dressed up too. He looked a little uncomfortable slouched against the wall.

"Hi," I said, not hiding my surprise.

"Hi, Leigh. You look beautiful. Do you know where we're going?" Did he say beautiful? Was he really talking to me? Maybe it was stress. He really seemed nervous.

"Are you coming with us? How fun. Hi, I'm Betsy," she smiled and waved.

He waved back, still looking tense. But still looking mostly at me. I wanted to stand closer to him, but I didn't know how without looking like I was, you know, trying to stand closer to him. Grammy came out of her room wearing a suit and exquisite sandals.

"Well, don't we all look gorgeous?" she said.

Betsy said, "Yes. Yes we do," and we all laughed.

"Just a few more minutes of suspense, darlings. Jump in the car, please." Grammy herded us out to the garage. Betsy sat up front with Grammy for the first time on this trip. Trevor opened the door for me (I saw that coming, or I wouldn't have waited) and I slid over to let him follow me. I guess he wasn't paying attention, because he came around the other side of the car and opened the other door.

"Oh, hello. Can I sit by you?" he whispered. I felt myself blushing again as I scooted back to the other seat. As he leaned over to buckle his seat belt, he whispered again, "Do you have any idea what's going on?"

I shrugged. Bending over my own seat belt, I answered, "I'm just along for the ride." His hand was on the seat between us, really close to me. Could I just reach over and take it? I wanted to wait a minute, to see if he'd leave it there. I picked an invisible piece of lint off my skirt and straightened my shirt under the seat belt. When I was finished fidgeting, I looked over at Trevor. He was watching me. Then I flicked my eyes to the rearview mirror. Grammy was watching me too. I shot her a little scowl, and her eyes returned to the road. But I could see her smiling. Betsy was sort of watching me as well, but mostly I think she was watching Trevor. She was turned in her seat so she could start a conversation, but she wasn't talking.

And I couldn't think of a thing to say. Which was bizarre, really, because my entire personality is about me always having something to say. Trevor's hand was still on the seat beside me, so I put mine there too, our fingers barely touching. My stomach hurt in a way that made me think that hurting felt good.

"Have you ever been to Oklahoma before?" Trevor asked Betsy. As she chattered her answer to him, one of his fingers slowly stroked mine. I could practically see steam rising off my skin. My lungs felt squeezed, like I couldn't get a whole breath. Part of me, the part that wanted oxygen, hoped this ride wouldn't last too long. But the other part, the part that thought breathing was overrated, was starting to think Texas wasn't a bad option.

~

"You have got to be kidding. Oh, Grammy. You are kidding, aren't you?" I whined. We were standing outside a community theater, where—you guessed it—*Oklahoma!* was showing. I really thought we had gotten past this tradition.

"It's Betsy's first trip. You wouldn't deny her this important part of our culture, would you?" Grammy winked and whispered, "Besides, you got the consolation prize."

"All is forgiven," I whispered back.

Bustling us into our seats, Grammy placed herself between Betsy and me, with Trevor on my other side. He settled into his seat and started reading the playbill.

"How many times have you done this?" I asked him.

"What, gone on a date with your grandma? Never."

"No," I laughed. "I mean, seen this show."

"I guess it's a day for first times. I've never seen it before."

I was shocked. "What? Are you serious? How can you live

here and never see this show? I'm sure it is being performed somewhere in the city at any time, all year."

He shrugged as the overture began. Grammy sighed and shifted in her seat. With the house lights down, Trevor reached for my hand. He leaned over and whispered, "Do you mind?"

"What? Seeing this show for the thirteenth time? Or seeing it with you?"

"I meant, um, I . . ."

I brought my other hand over so I was holding his hand in both of mine. "I know. I really, really don't mind," I said.

It's possible that this was the best version of *Oklahoma!* ever produced. I certainly didn't notice any mistakes or flaws. But maybe my attention was just a little diverted. Maybe. At intermission, Betsy asked me to help her find the rest room.

"Is he holding your hand?"

"Not at the moment." Why did I sound so defensive?

"He's beautiful, isn't he?" Oh, good. She approved. Yippee. I just nodded. What was wrong with me? Why didn't I want to talk to her about Trevor? Because I felt stupid. I felt like she was patronizing me. Like she was a great artist, and she was applauding me for my first attempt at finger painting. Why did I have to keep going back to this insecurity? Why did I let myself believe she was always on the attack? I didn't say anything else to her during the break or as we found our way back to our seats.

Through the second act I was tense. I felt stupid about being mad at Betsy for trying to be interested in my fling. Maybe she was just being nice. Was it possible for me to have an uncomplicated reaction to anything she did? Why did I always have to look for motives? I could tell, walking back from the rest room with her at intermission, that I'd hurt her with my silence. But I didn't know what else to do. Would it have been better if she hadn't said anything? Would I have liked it better if she'd acted like she didn't care?

I was so uptight during the second act that I was sitting forward in my chair, hands clenched on my knees. After at least half an hour, I realized that I must have been sending a serious body-language message to Trevor. I leaned back in my seat and turned to him. "Hi," I whispered. He had his arms folded across his chest.

"Did I do something wrong?" he asked. "Sorry if I did."

Holy cow. What a sweet guy. "No, not at all. Betsy and I just had a little . . ." what? Not an argument, not a fight. Not even a moment. "Sometimes we just have a hard time. I think I was a jerk to her. Sorry it came across like that."

"So you're okay?"

Nodding, I felt his arm go over my shoulder. Oh, yeah. I was okay. I snuggled into his shoulder and had no idea what was going on up on stage until the end of the play. As the last song began, the audience stood together. I dragged Trevor up out of his seat as Grammy pulled Betsy to her feet. Trevor looked at me, confused.

"Hand on your heart," I whispered as the whole room sang along with Curly.

"Ohhhhh-klahoma, where the wind comes sweeping down the plain . . ."

It always cracked me up to see this part. The whole audience, on their feet, held their hands to their hearts and belted out the state's song. I snuck a glance at Betsy to see how she was taking it. She was laughing, but in a nice way. Everything she did really was in a nice way, because she was a nice girl. I wished that I could just give her credit for being sincere and honest. I knew she was trying harder than I was. I kept glancing at her until I caught her eye. She smiled while she sang, and I tried to look apologetic as I smiled back.

"You're doing fine, Oklahoma. Oklahoma, OK!" Would we ever be fine? Would I ever let us be okay?

Chapter 12

Trevor came over the next day. I heard the knock, and then his voice, and tried to be casual as I hurried to the door. He was talking to Grammy, but when I got there, he stopped. I should have waited. I wanted to know what he said when I wasn't around. He was holding a paper lunch sack.

"Hi. Are you busy?" he asked.

"No. We're just hanging out. What's up?"

He held up the bag. "Want to see the baby ducks?"

"Please," I begged, "tell me you don't have baby ducks in that."

He laughed. "No. They're in the creek. But we have to distract the bigger ducks somehow. They love my mom's cooking, too." He shook the sack like he was dangling a prize.

"See you later, Peach. Bye, Trev," Grammy called as she walked away into the kitchen. She couldn't have made it more obvious that she wanted me to go.

It was a perfect day. The sun was bright, but not too hot. Flowers bloomed everywhere, trees were shading the sidewalks, and a light breeze blew around us.

"The end of April is a perfect time to come to Oklahoma,"

I said to Trevor. "Hey, did anyone ever tell you that you don't look like a Trevor?"

"You mean besides the entire Tongan side of my family? Nope. It's never come up." He smiled at me and took my hand. In full daylight. In his neighborhood. "My dad had a brother who died really young. His name was Trevor, so I'm like a built-in memory of him. He was blond and wore glasses and liked to play chess, or so the story goes. I'm exactly like him, don't you think?"

"What happened to him?" I was being nosy, but mostly I just wanted to keep him talking.

"He was in a car accident," Trevor said simply.

I sort of gasped and took my hand away to cover my mouth. "How awful," I whispered. I felt all the color leave my face.

Trevor looked concerned and put his arm around my shoulders. "Hey, sorry. I didn't mean to upset you. He's, you know, okay now," he said. I must have looked confused, because he added, "I mean, it doesn't hurt him anymore. You know, where he is."

Not too eager to get into a big existential afterlife discussion right now, I just nodded. He reached for my hand again and said, "You're shaking. Are you okay?"

"Sure. So where are these ducks?" I tried to keep the flutter out of my voice.

We wandered through the neighborhood and crossed a little bridge over a creek. On the other side were huge, flat rocks. We climbed down and sat near the water. Trevor said we just had to wait a minute and they'd come. I was glad to be sitting. My hands were still shaking, so I tucked them under my knees. He sat close to me, leaning back on his arms. I could tell he was watching me.

"Leigh, I'm really sorry for whatever I said that upset you. Are you going to be okay?"

So much for me hiding my emotions. "I'm good. Fine. Sorry about that. I was in a car accident once, and it still gives me a little bit of a freak-out. Sorry."

"What happened?" he asked.

"You know what? I'd really rather not talk about it." I was staring at my shoes.

"Oh. Okay. Hey, here come the ducks."

Perfect timing. Seven tiny puffballs were floating along behind a brown duck with a white star on her head. They were making the kind of almost-chirp the twins made when they tried to whistle. They were so cute and noisy. Each one couldn't have been making much of a sound, but all together, it was a little symphony of squeaking.

Trevor put his hand on my back. "Good to see you smiling. Here. See if they're hungry." I wondered what form of barbecued Tongan food these ducks were used to, but as Trevor handed me the bag, I pulled out animal crackers.

"Did your mom cook these up this morning?" I teased.

"You have to give them something plain. Otherwise they'll get hooked on my mom's food and never be satisfied with stale bread again. They'll follow the scent of the grill right to my backyard and move in. They'll never leave. I've actually been hoping you would come over and eat something she makes. Then maybe you'd stay too."

He turned to sit in front of me and I felt my face go hot. Still leaning on one arm, he put his other hand on my shoulder. He started drawing little circles with his finger, and my arm tingled all the way down to my fingernails. I looked down at my knees to be sure I was still there. Glancing back up at him, I was amazed how he was staring at me. Like he was trying to memorize me. Did I really care why? Did it matter? I was being *adored*. He moved his hand from my shoulder to my face. His fingers barely touched my cheek, slid down my jaw-line, and grazed my mouth.

I kissed his finger.

That was ridiculously forward of me. All the muscles in my stomach and arms had turned to jelly. His hand was in my hair, right at the base of my neck, and I felt his breath on my cheek as he moved closer. It was too much work to stay vertical *and* keep my eyes open, so I closed my eyes. The tiny squeaking ducklings got very loud. Trevor's cheek was against mine. I could smell soap and feel his breath in my ear. I stifled an urge to twitch—I have an ear thing. Then he sort of slid his face across mine as he turned his head.

I could feel his curls against my forehead as he rested his head on mine. This was taking a very long time, which was great, because pretty soon it would all be over and I would never again have this moment, this pre-kiss excitement. I breathed in the smells around us—mostly *his*—and tried hard to memorize every sensation.

The kiss was tender. He had great lips, full and gentle. I reached up my hand, and the thought crossed my mind that I could tell Betsy that I'd touched his hair. I felt his mouth move, and I could tell he was smiling. I smiled too, and then I laughed because I was worried that our teeth would crash together.

"What's so funny?" But he was laughing too.

Then I heard a splash and we both looked at the stream in

time to see the mama duck drag the paper sack full of animal crackers into the water.

"Now what?" he said.

"You're asking me? I don't know. Will the paper bag kill them? Will they be able to get the cookies out? Is it just going to sink?" I was panicky, but not really about the ducklings.

Trevor looked at me out of the corner of his eye and stood up. He walked over to the edge of the water, picked up the wet bag, dumped the crackers, and shoved the sack into his pocket. Then he came back with a grin on his face, put out his hand, and pulled me up. Apparently we were going for a walk. If I could manage to remember how.

Coming up the driveway a couple of hours later, hands full of Grammy's junk mail, I overheard Betsy playing Grammy's piano. I glanced through the window screen and found Grammy leaning against the side of the piano, humming along. It was her favorite kind of music to sing along to—in her secret heart, Grammy always wished she could have been a Broadway sensation.

Propped open in front of Betsy was what I sweetly referred to as "The Great Big Book of Cheesy Broadway Musical Numbers," which, under torture, I would confess that I love. I guess last night's trip to Musical Heaven had inspired them. The book was chock-full of the best of the best (which I would never, under normal, nontorture circumstances, admit knowing): Rodgers and Hammerstein, Lerner and Lowe, Webber, Sondheim, and on and on. So on and on Betsy played.

Grammy scooted from her corner of the piano to the bench, snuggled up close to Betsy. She also advanced from humming to full-throated belting. I had snuck in the front door unnoticed, and stood against the wall wishing for a camera. Mom used to say, "My heart is taking a picture," and I know mine did then. They were having so much fun that I couldn't interrupt.

Betsy's hand came around Grammy's back to hit some of those really high notes in a "deedly-deedly" big finish. She squeezed Grammy around her shoulders and kissed her cheek.

"That was beautiful," Betsy sighed. "Thank you for singing to me. And thank you for bringing me here. You've been so nice to me, and so welcoming. Your home is a golden-yellow, happy, wonderful place."

Grammy was charmed, delighted by Betsy's graciousness. I wished I knew how to say so much with so little language. And I felt good about sharing Grammy. She could like Betsy and still love me as much as she ever had. I closed the door behind me and said, "Does anyone want to know what I just did?"

A few days into our whirlwind tour of Fascinating Oklahoma City, I started feeling antsy. I couldn't really explain it; I was twitchy, uncomfortable. Something was not right. It wasn't anything about Trevor. That was pretty comfortable. Better than comfortable: yummy. I was invited to dinner the next night—we all were. As evening came on, Betsy and I sat on the deck (Grammy couldn't insist I call it the "verandah" when she was inside on the phone) listening to the creek trickle by.

"How come there are no mosquitoes?" Betsy asked.

Maybe I meant to distress her; maybe I was just having one of my fits of snottiness. I just told her. No warning. No grace. "Bats."

Betsy let a fairly bad word escape and ducked in her seat. "Where?"

Casually, I pointed to a wooden contraption in the eaves. "Bat house. You can buy them at the hardware store here, just like a birdhouse. Bats eat the mosquitoes and go back home. They almost never need to nest in people's hair." I found a perverse pleasure in watching her squirm.

Grammy, apparently finished with her business on the phone, joined us with a plate of snacks. Noticing Betsy's altered posture and fierce protection of her hair, she decided to make small talk. "Have you met Chuckles?"

As if on cue, a demonic laugh sounded from the tree over our heads.

Very bad word. Twice.

"What was that?" Betsy squeaked.

"Well, darling, you're referring either to my owl or to your own purple curse. I'll assume it's the former. Chuckles nests in this tree and keeps me company at night." Turning to me, Grammy asked, "Comes from sailor stock, does she?"

Uncharacteristically sensitive at the moment, I told her Betsy was just unaccustomed to the wildlife. "City girl." I smiled at Betsy to assure her it was okay.

"Maybe you'd better pray the possums don't come out tonight. We might lose her."

As Betsy regained her composure over pita chips and hummus, I was again feeling uneasy. Grammy, watching me fiddle with her snacks, recognized the signs.

"What's troubling you, gumdrop?"

"I don't know; just a feeling. A sense—maybe a premonition. Can living in your house for half a week make me psychic?" I joked.

"The psychic force in my home predicts only joy and pleasure. You just don't like the hummus."

Assuring her the dip was heavenly, I tried to shake off the uncomfortable mist in my mind. No deal. "Do you care if I call my mom?"

"Go ahead, sweet one. Betsy and I will try to keep the vicious gossip about you and Trevor to a minimum while you're gone." Grammy smiled innocently and fluttered her eyelashes, and I turned heavily into the house. What was wrong with me?

"Hey, Mom." I tried and failed to keep the depressed tone out of my voice.

"Oh, honey. So you've heard. Are you okay?"

All the blood in my body rushed straight to my face. I thought I might melt the phone.

"What have I heard? I'm okay. I think I'm okay. What's going on?" Panic settled in.

"Oh, baby. Sorry. You need to call Jeremy. Everything's fine. Just give him a call."

"What? What's going on? Tell." Whining and pleading never worked with her, but instinct was instinct, after all.

"Call me back after you've talked to Germ. I love you, babe." Click. Nice.

"Hi, Mrs. Bentley. It's Leigh. Sorry to bother you. Is Jeremy home? He's not answering his cell." Time to breathe. In, out. In again.

"Sure, hon. I think he's in the shower. Hang on a minute. He really wants to talk to you."

Over the awkward sounds of Jeremy's mom getting his attention mid-shower, I heard the blood rushing through my ears. Whatever this was, I could hear about it after he dried and dressed, for heaven's sake.

"Mrs. Bentley?" I tried to get her attention, but she was obviously trying to shield my ears from the shower sounds. I heard her muffled holler and fully expected Jeremy to bring her to her senses—he really could call me back. But the clunk of the shower turning off was followed almost indecently closely by Germ's voice. I had the distinctly uncomfortable suspicion that I was now in the shower. With him. In a way. You know.

"Hey, Leigh. How are you?"

"Moderately freaked out. Are you in the shower?"

"Hold, please." Pause. "Okay, I have full towel coverage. All better now?"

"I'm not sure. I think I'm getting gray hair and ulcers. Everyone's gone crazy—at least both our mothers. What is going on?"

"Okay, well, I've been thinking all day about how to tell you this, because it's not . . . um, well, it's a little . . . hmm. See, I . . . hmm. Okay?"

"Totally. Okay. Good night."

A little laugh. "Right. So. I just . . . today was . . . I had to . . ."

"Sweet Jeremy, you are my very best friend, but I may hate you soon. You are driving me insane. Is or is not everything all right?" I was sure he could hear my heartbeat through the phone.

"Pretty much all right, except I had to go in to the clinic and I got my test results today, and it's back."

Oh.

Oh, no.

What do you say to your best friend from hundreds of miles away to convey your horror and distress that the leukemia that poisons his blood is on another rampage? I felt my stomach turn to water. My brain rushed around to get a grip on this hideous news.

"Oh. Oh. Oh. Germ, I've got nothing. Oh. I'm so . . ."

Horrified. Frightened. Far away. Sick. Guilty. Shocked. Very, very sad. I had the strange feeling that this was my fault. At the same time I had become distracted by Trevor, Jeremy's body had betrayed him. Did that mean I had betrayed him too?

"What can I do? How can I help you?"

"Thanks. I don't know much yet. But there is one huge thing you can do for me."

Anything. Whatever you ask. "What?"

"I want you to tell Betsy for me," his voice cracked, "because I don't want to. Because I know you'll do it gently. Because . . ." I could hear his breathing change, and I knew I was listening to the sound of a heart breaking. Knowing him as well as I did, I knew he wasn't crying for his pain, or his sickness, or his mortality, or his fear. He was mourning what this would do to Betsy. His heart was breaking for her.

"I will tell her right now if you want me to. Do you have details you want me to give her?" I couldn't come right out and ask if they'd given him an expiration date. I felt my breath catch, and the tears came.

"Just give her the gist. She doesn't know anything. I haven't told her about any of this. Just be . . . you know."

"Mm-hm." I didn't trust myself with words—I was still feigning control of my emotions.

He sighed and sniffed. "I'm so sorry to do this to you. I hate to give you all this. But I know you guys can help each other out. Thank you. I love you, Leigh."

"I love you, too, Jeremy. Good night," I whispered.

After I'd hung up, I realized that I hadn't even thought of telling him about Trevor. There would be enough time for that later, right?

He knew I'd tell her gently. Gently? Come on. How gentle could I be? And honestly, what did he expect me to say? So I just bucked up and went back outside. As soon as they saw me, Betsy and Grammy knew that something big was wrong. I sat on the floor by Grammy's feet and laid my head on her knees. Time to dive in.

"In eighth grade Jeremy got sick. It started with knee trouble so bad he had to quit track. Then his knee hurt so much that walking was painful. He sort of limped around for a while. The doctors gave it some hideous name—rhabdo-something sarcoma. Cancer. He had to do chemo, surgery, radiation, all of it. It was brutal. He was so sick. He got totally skinny because nothing tasted good, not even chocolate. For weeks he could eat nothing but soup. He lost all his hair and got nasty, awful sores all over. I have never seen anyone so sick. The sickness lasted for months. I honestly couldn't fathom what the cancer must be like if the cure was this hideous. Then it was gone. Cancer free. The hair came back. The sores healed. Food was good. He was fixed, and I was so grateful for that horrible radiation and whatever else the doctors made him go through, because it helped. It cleaned him up and made him perfect again. For two years I believed that. Then, hey, here's some wonderful news: Radiation can cause cancer.

"Talk about ironies. His radiation treatments gave him leukemia. It doesn't happen very often, but it happened to him. More nightmare treatments. More sickness. This was right after my dad died, and now I was sure I was losing my best friend, too. But Jeremy kept up his perfect attitude through all that mess, just like you'd expect him to. He was always worried about everyone else, making sure we were all okay. He'd check up on me and Mom and the girls, and he used to have me come over and rub his head for luck. He helped me work through . . . some stuff, and all the time he was fighting off rampaging white cells. He's been amazing and brave and then finally healthy, and now it's come back. He's sick again. He . . . he wanted me to tell you."

I finally raised my head enough to look at Betsy. Her face was waxy pale. She looked very much as if she'd like to vomit. Slowly and shakily she stood up from the rocker and sank to the floor next to me, our knees touching, her head near Grammy's other knee. Grammy's hands rested in our hair, and she stroked our heads gently. Night sounds settled around us as we sat together, letting the tears come.

The human heart has four chambers. Just one of the lovely and fairly useless nuggets of physiological wisdom I've gleaned over the years in the Indianapolis public school system. So here's the thing—could a person turn one of them off? If it stopped working or got broken, could it be ignored? Could surgeons and scientists uncover a way to function on three? And if a girl had the need, could she maybe learn to shut down another one before it totally broke?

Chapter 13

Because she's a lady of class and has a perfectly gracious nature, Grammy pretended to believe that Betsy and I would like nothing better than to spend the next four days in our sweats eating ice cream and watching old musicals on cable. She must have known we were hiding from the world, hiding from reality, but she kept the treats coming and sat behind us on the couch for hours. She even made an excuse to Trevor, who came only once and then quietly disappeared back into the house next door.

Grammy would brush our hair, scratch our backs, sing along with the films, and wait for us to want to talk. She'd be waiting a while. Betsy was too busy crying and writing in that journal of hers to speak.

And me? I couldn't figure what to say. How could I make it any better by talking more about it? Jeremy was sick, really sick, and discussing it wouldn't make him feel better. It certainly wouldn't make *me* feel better. And the less Betsy knew about this awful business, the better for her. So I spent a couple of days in relative and uncharacteristic silence.

I felt myself going fuzzy around the edges—I was losing

touch with my own details. I recognized that as a symptom of the way I grieve. You know, some people cry a lot (Betsy, apparently), some talk through everything (Mom, Jeremy, Grammy—strangely, all the truly emotionally healthy people I know), and some of us wrap a blanket of oblivion and disbelief around ourselves as everything goes cloudy. I realize that the world still goes on, but I give it permission to go on without my input. As far as professional opinion was concerned, I understood this was not an acceptable form of dealing with grief. I simply chose not to care about professional opinion.

Late one evening, I woke in front of the TV with Audrey Hepburn lip-synching to Rex Harrison (who didn't deserve her, let's be honest) and Betsy's mane of honey-blonde, silky, matted (?) dirty (?!) and ratty (?!?) hair was mashed into my shoulder. My first thought as I clawed through the cobwebs of sleep and emotional denial was that she was seriously just way too close. But as I located my own feet (easily accomplished by drawing a visual line away from my waist), I discovered to my growing embarrassment that I had flung an entire leg over Betsy in my sleep. Major IPS (Invasion of Personal Space). I tried to lift my leg away without waking her, but my rear end was completely useless as a muscle group. Needles and stars shot through my leg from toes to hip, triggering an uncontrollable full-body twitch.

Unsurprisingly, this affected Betsy's snooze. She shot up from my shoulder and we crashed heads. Giggles from the couch behind us informed me that Grammy had watched the whole thing.

"Ow. Leigh, you've got a head like a bowling ball."

"Mmm. Thankth. I think I bit my tongue in half."

Grammy casually came to our aid with an iced drink of questionable origin. Without sitting up from her comfortable reclining position, she said, "Please don't drink it, just rest it between your lumpy heads. And keep it down, will you? This is my favorite movie."

These were the words she said at the beginning of each film in the marathon of self-pity in which we were indulging. Which was funny, really, because neither Betsy nor I had been saying much of anything for several days. Leaning her head on the cold glass that I held, Betsy started to laugh. Her shoulders shook. Her laughter snuck out her nose in little huffs, which of course cracked me up. Trying to laugh silently should be an Olympic sport, because it takes great control and stamina. Neither of which I have, apparently. I tried to keep my lips closed, thinking that would keep me silent. But my eyes started leaking, and whatever Grammy had been drinking sloshed over the brim of the glass into my stinky hair. A puttering, squeaky noise escaped my nearly closed lips, and I just lost it. I tried to hand Grammy back her drink, but dumped it on the couch.

"Good thing I went for the leather," she muttered, and Betsy fell over on the floor laughing. I offered Grammy a corner of my blanket to sop up her drink, but it was useless, as the blanket was fleece. Grammy rolled her eyes as Betsy and I gasped for breath on the living-room floor. The floodgates were opened, and we let days of pent-up and blocked emotion come out in laughter. It wasn't long before the laughter brought tears—first the laughing kind, and then the real kind. We sat on the floor, sobbing and shaking. I wrapped my knees in my arms and bawled, my face hidden in my sweatpants. Grammy stroked my head as I moaned loudly—like a little kid. When I realized what a racket I was making, I looked up at Grammy and laughed at myself. What a relief.

Betsy wiped her eyes and leaned over to hug me. I held her shoulders and tried to catch my breath.

"You know, we should really try to make it to a shower tomorrow. Your hair smells awful," she said.

"Thanks. You, though. You look better than I've ever seen you. I think you should always go days without hygiene. And the swollen red eyes, this is a great look for you," I said, wiping my nose on my shirt sleeve.

Grammy snorted and turned up the volume. Betsy put her head back on my shoulder and shuddered a sigh as we prepared to sing along with Rex and Audrey.

I'm happy to report that we did rediscover soap and shampoo the day before we left Oklahoma. Our explosion of laughter and tears the night before was enough to convince Grammy that we would, in time, become emotionally healthy. Or at least we could be open; she decided nothing else really needed to be said about the Jeremy situation.

After a last-night celebration dinner at Bellini's (fettuccini alfredo with bacon, in a bowl twice the size of my head), we settled back on the verandah for night-bird song and relaxing conversation. I needed to tell Grammy how glad I was that I'd come.

"Grammy, I'm glad we came." Did I say *we?* I meant *I.*

But I guess I also meant *we.* It had been fun to play dress-up and makeover with Betsy and Grammy. And I loved showing off my Grammy to Betsy. And if there had been no Betsy to keep Grammy company, I might have felt a little guilty running off to have my first fling. And I was not regretting my fling. And if Betsy had been at home when Jeremy's test results had come back, he might have called her instead of me. And she could have been there and cried on his shoulder, and they would have comforted each other, and then maybe she would have called me, or maybe she wouldn't have, and maybe I still wouldn't know anything going on with him, and no matter how awful it was, I still needed to know, and so maybe I was really glad we came. Was it all right to want her with me just so she wouldn't be with him? Whatever. "I'm really glad we came."

———

I tossed my suitcase into Grammy's trunk and walked next door. Trevor's yard was nicely kept. I wondered if he got paid to do that, too. Probably not. Do people pay their own kids to do yard work?

Taking a deep breath, I knocked. As though someone had been watching, the door swung open immediately and I was scooped up by a woman with a wooden spoon in her hand.

"You must be Leigh. Hi, honey."

"Um, hi, Mrs. . . ." Oh, how embarrassing. I didn't even know Trevor's last name. Her smile told me she knew exactly what I was feeling. But she didn't supply any information.

"Come in. Let me get you a drink. Do you have a few minutes? How about a snack?" I remembered what Trevor had told me about his mom's propensity to feed people.

"Thanks. I have a couple of minutes before I head to the airport. Is Trevor at home?"

She handed me a glass of lemonade and nodded. But she

didn't call for him or make any move to go get him. Putting her arm around my shoulder, she spoke in a deep voice, "I'm so sorry to hear about your friend's illness. I bet you can't wait to get home, huh?"

I found myself completely at ease with this total stranger. I wanted to be honest. "I'm torn," I said simply.

"Tell me," she said, as if she knew I would.

"I want to get home and make sure things are okay. I want to see my family and my friend. But I'll miss my Grammy and," could I say it? Why not? "And Trevor. He's been great."

"My Trevor is a fantastic kid. And he thinks a lot of you."

I looked at her, hoping she'd go on. Did she mean that he thought about me a lot? Or that what he thought about me was good? But she didn't offer any specifics. She just put a plate of chicken in front of me and handed me a napkin. Not a fork. Did I mention that it was 10:30 in the morning?

The chicken smelled great, but I wasn't sure I could eat it. For one thing, I'd never eaten chicken with skin on it. The idea of it really grossed me out under normal circumstances. Also, it was huge. A drumstick and a thigh, still connected in a long, hinged chunk. Meat on bones was something else I didn't do well. It was too hard to ignore that an animal had once used this to walk around with. I was obviously supposed to just pick it up and tear into it.

Just as I was feeling the beginnings of panic, Trevor walked into the kitchen. Apparently he had just gotten out of bed, because he was shirtless and messy-haired. I really didn't want to dwell on this, but the sight of him right then was a picture I'd carry home with me. He kissed his mom and mumbled,

"Morning." He still hadn't seen me there, standing against the counter. His mom elbowed him and nodded toward me.

He was totally shocked to see me. And for me to see him, I guess. He bolted out of the kitchen, returning long enough to stick his head around the corner and say, "Please don't leave." I nodded and he ran—presumably for a shirt. Or a toothbrush. Maybe both.

His mom stood smiling at me from her end of the kitchen while I leaned on the counter not eating chicken. I was feeling pretty guilty with the silence and the food on my plate, and I decided if I'd been brave with Trevor, I could be brave with his mom.

"I'm sorry. I'm a little nervous. I don't think I can eat now. Do you mind?" I asked, pointing to the dish next to me.

"Not at all, honey. Let me wrap it up for you." She opened a cupboard full of Styrofoam take-out containers and started stuffing food into one as she hummed in her low voice. Now it was not just the one enormous chicken part—it got company. More meat, some kind of salad, and something I could not identify that looked like it was made with mayonnaise. I tried to smile graciously, but the sight of all that food made the butterflies in my stomach do a complicated dance. I couldn't think of anything else to say to this lovely, comforting woman, so I just watched as she did her thing.

It wasn't long before Trevor returned to the kitchen. He was wearing jeans and a T-shirt, and the edges of his hair were wet, like they'd gotten in the way when he washed his face. He looked a little shy, or maybe embarrassed, but asked me if I'd go outside with him.

Taking my hand, he led me to a chair on the patio and

brought another to face me so when he sat, our knees touched. He leaned forward and held both my hands. "Hi," he whispered. "I've missed you." We just looked at each other for a while. Then he said, "I didn't think I'd get to see you again. I mean, today—before you have to leave. Is everything okay? I really didn't get any details. I mean, I know it's none of my business," he hurried on, "and if you don't want to talk about it, that's cool."

"Thanks. It's probably going to get ugly pretty soon, but things shouldn't have changed too much by this afternoon when I get home." I took a deep breath. "It's weird to have a friend who is really sick. It's hard to leave a room he's in. I don't like to say goodnight. I have to fight a constant urge to give him things, because even though I know it's stupid, I want him to be surrounded by things that remind him of me."

Trevor laughed. "Sorry. That's not really funny, except that I have spent the last four days deciding to give you a present, and then deciding not to, and then thinking I will, and then thinking I won't."

"So where did you leave it? Are you going to give me something?" I teased.

"Yeah. It's inside. In the kitchen. It's this big container of chicken and stuff."

We laughed and he pulled me to my feet. Wrapping me up in his arms, he held me and we sort of rocked back and forth. After a couple of minutes, Trevor whispered into my hair, "I'm so sorry about your friend. I wish it could be easy for you, and for him, and for everyone."

I reached my hands up around his neck and smiled at him, even though I was close to tears. "Thanks, Trevor. That's really sweet of you. But I only have a couple of minutes before I have to leave, and I didn't really come over here to talk about Jeremy."

"Really? I'm very glad to hear that," he said, leaning down to kiss my cheek.

"You have been great. You're great. I mean, this has been great." Where had my brain gone? "Sorry. I'm turning dumb. But thanks. For, you know, everything. Especially the chicken in the kitchen."

After a very pleasant few minutes of no talking, Trevor said, "Come back and visit soon. Your grandma will miss you, you know."

"I'll be back."

"I'm counting on it," he smiled.

Chapter 14

Unloading our bags from the luggage carousel, I glanced around for Mom or Paul. Not finding either, I told Betsy I'd try them on the paging phone while she hit the ladies' room. As I neared the stand of telephones, I heard a pinched, metallic voice call, "Doctor Leigh Mason, please pick up a white paging phone. Doctor Leigh Mason, please pick up a white paging phone." Jeremy was here.

I grabbed a phone and almost simultaneously felt a tap on my shoulder. Stuffing the phone back on its cradle, I flung myself at Jeremy. With my arms around his neck, I felt tears pricking at my eyes. It was a relief to be close to him, to be able to touch, to see, to smell, to feel his arms around me. I wanted to drink him in and pass him all my healthy cells and cancer-free vibes.

"How was the trip? There's a neighbor I need to hear about."

"You'll hear all about it. Not now. I need the proper atmosphere. Maybe someplace warm and steamy." I wiggled my eyebrows and we both laughed.

"Did you have any weather adventures?" He always asked

that. As if huge thunderstorms and tornados didn't happen in Indianapolis too.

"Nope. We had a bit of rain, and it did get a little soggy inside the house, if you can imagine," I hinted, wiping an imaginary tear from my cheek.

"How did she do?" he asked.

"Grammy? She was sad, but not totally surprised. She said to give you her love and to tell you that strawberry crepes with whipped cream have remarkable healing properties."

"Okay, thanks for that. I meant Betsy, dummy."

"About like you'd expect. I'm happy to report that she does, in fact, like you very much—enough to soggy up Grammy's guest-room pillows and run through several boxes of tissue. You'll be terribly proud of me for the way I handled the whole thing, I must say. I was gentle and thorough and knowledge-able and sensitive, just like you had anticipated me to be." I grinned at him, thinking I would get a laugh, but not so much. He just leaned against the phone box and looked at me.

"Of course you were," he murmured quietly. "I knew you would be."

He glanced up, and I turned to see what had caught his attention. Betsy stood in the center of the baggage claim area scanning for a familiar face. Jeremy lit up and flagged her over. Expecting her to run at him (in an entirely different way than I had recently run at him, of course), I was surprised to see her take a minute to adjust her bag over her shoulder, check the wheels on her suitcase, and slowly walk toward us, looking mostly at the floor. Jeremy glanced at me with raised eyebrows, and I shrugged my confusion.

"Hey, welcome home." He put his arm around her as she

made brief eye contact. She raised her eyes again and tried to smile at him, with dismal result. He reached for both our suitcases and quickly shot me a hurt look.

Walking to the car, Betsy remained a step behind me, and when Jeremy slowed to walk beside her, she came around on my other side. In silence he popped the trunk and lifted our bags inside. Betsy clutched her carry-on to her chest like a flotation device. You don't need a scientific degree to read body language like that. Staring at me meaningfully, she gave a little nod toward the front door. I was clueless.

"What?" I mouthed to her.

"You sit in the front. Please?" she mouthed back.

I shrugged my assent. No problem. In I went.

She climbed in the backseat directly behind Jeremy. Strategic move to make it hard for him to see her in the mirror, I figured. I just couldn't tell why. Maybe she was planning a crying jag for the ride home.

Pulling on my seat belt, I could see Jeremy standing by the now-closed trunk, clearly taking deep breaths.

"What is going on?" I whisper-hissed. "What's the matter with you?"

She looked over the seat, pale, scared, and sickish. "Nothing. Leave it," she muttered as Jeremy slid in.

Faking a Pakistani taxi driver accent and a cheerful face, Jeremy asked, "Where to, ladies?" I could tell he was hoping for some time with Betsy, but she wasn't buying it.

"Home, James," I said, suddenly feeling ripped in half. I wanted Jeremy to go away so I could talk to Betsy, figure out what was going on. She looked so strange, like she was afraid of Jeremy. She hadn't said a word to him, and she avoided his eyes, even through the rearview mirror. I couldn't figure her out. Wasn't she glad to see him?

And, for his part, Germ looked like he could seriously use a hug. So part of me wanted Betsy gone so I could make him all right. His shoulders slumped and he seemed to have forgotten his smile, which was normally so obvious. He casually moved the mirror so he could see Betsy, but she hid her face behind her hair as she stared out the window. He moved the mirror back, took a bracing breath, and glanced at me.

"So, tell me what you guys have been up to," he said, offering me an opening to smooth over the growing discomfort. I chattered about our trip, hinted that Grammy had some very interesting neighbors, ran on about the backyard wildlife, about pedicures and good food and cheesy musicals, until we reached our driveway, allowing Betsy and Jeremy to sink inside their private moods. As long as I kept talking, I didn't have to choose between making Jeremy uncomfortable and making Betsy cry.

The twins had put up a banner across the garage door, a welcome home sign with four partially deflated balloons affixed to the vinyl with duct tape. Dad would have been proud. Duct tape is a man's best friend, he used to say.

As soon as the car was in park, Betsy vaulted from her door. "I've got to . . ."

She couldn't use the bathroom excuse; we'd both seen her come out of it seventeen minutes ago. She apparently recognized this and didn't even try to finish her sentence. She just ran up the steps and into the house.

Still in my seat belt, I looked over at Jeremy. "Want to stay?" I asked.

"Let me get your bags inside, then I'd better go," he smiled sadly.

"Wait, Germ. How are you doing? Are you, you know, feeling okay?"

He shook his head and his hair fell into his eyes. Time for a haircut, again. "I felt great half an hour ago. What's up with her? What happened?"

"Honestly, I have no idea. How about you pretend everything is fine and we still love you, and I'll call you when it's true. I'll find out what's going on."

I waved good-bye as he pulled out of the driveway and into the street. Too fast.

The house was quiet. Everyone else must have assumed, like I had, like Jeremy had, that we wouldn't be back quite so soon.

Betsy was on her bed in fetal position, face against the wall.

"Exactly what was that all about back there?" I demanded in my gentle, tactful way.

No response.

"Hello? What were you going for? Because the part of excited, happy girlfriend went unperformed."

"Excited, happy girlfriend," Betsy repeated in a flat voice. "Oh, I'm excited, all right. Can't you just see it in my face."

I didn't get it. "I don't get it. What's up? Why are you acting so different? Nothing's changed."

Betsy stared at me with utter disbelief stamped across her forehead. "Nothing has changed? What are you saying? Everything has changed. I left Indianapolis nine days ago with a healthy, perfect boyfriend."

(I wanted so much to say, *well, you didn't actually leave with him,* but I knew what she was trying to say, so I held it in. Hey, a filter!)

"Now I come home and everything is different," she was saying, "and he's got some hideous sickness and you two act as if it's not there and I'm just supposed to ignore it too and pretend everything is peachy. Hello, Leigh. He has cancer. Leukemia. Don't you just feel your skin crawl to hear those ugly words? Jeremy is sick, really sick. Everything is *not* the same. I am not up for this." As soon as those last words were out of her mouth, Betsy gasped and covered her face. She clearly could not believe what she had just heard herself say.

Just like I'd felt in the car, I was torn. I hadn't known whom to protect, so I had just talked on and on so nobody had to be uneasy. Now I couldn't decide whether to focus on comforting her or defending him. So I stood there. Quietly. Waiting. Yeah, weird.

"Sorry," she eventually peeped. Sitting up, she patted the bed beside her. I sat. "That was a really stupid thing to say. You aren't up for this thing either, and Jeremy certainly can't be. That was selfish and shallow of me. But really, Leigh, aren't you scared? Doesn't this whole cancer thing just make you want to hide from the world, and from Jeremy especially? Aren't you afraid you'll hurt him? He doesn't need any more hurt now."

"You mean," I asked quietly, "like the kind of hurt you feel when someone you like very much turns away from you when you need her?"

She looked at me. "Do you think that's what I was doing? Turning away?"

"I just finish telling Jeremy how much you like him, how great he is for you, how perfect this whole relationship thing is, and you come out of the little girls' room avoiding him like a leper. You don't look at him, you won't speak to him—I'm sure he expected at least that much courtesy, if not a decent kiss after a week and a half apart. I tell him everything is lovely, and then you show up and make me a liar. Worse than that, I look mean. Like I've played a trick on him. I look stupid, you look like a jerk, and Germ feels horrible. Pretty good day."

"So what do I do now?" She was asking me? What did I know about this kind of thing?

"Well, first I think we both need a bowl of ice cream. Then you probably ought to call him and tell him how you feel."

"I'm totally up for the ice cream. But I don't think I can talk to him now."

"What if I call him and have him come over? What if he's here with both of us? Could you muster up some general courtesy? Will you speak when spoken to? Can you manage eye contact? Nobody's asking you to sit on his lap. Just be polite. Can you give it a try?"

"I don't know, Leigh. I'm scared."

"What are you scared of?" I wanted to go on, making a list of all the dumb things to feel and then telling her why they were dumb. But something stopped me—a realization that she had a right to feel however she needed to feel. And that I had had years to come to grips with Jeremy's cancer, on and off, whereas she was still getting through the initial shock.

"I'm scared of him. I'm scared that he'll be different now. Weak, sick, depressed, whatever. That he won't be who he has been, and that I won't like him anymore. And what kind of girl stops liking someone because he's sick? I'm scared that I'll accidentally hurt him. I'm scared of me. What if I'm not tough enough to handle being girlfriend to an ill person? What if I hate hospitals? Because I do hate hospitals. I feel like barfing every time I go inside. I'm even scared of you, because you will handle all this perfectly, in your way, and I won't, and Jeremy will realize you are the one he really cares about, and I was just a phase, and he will decide that whatever he has left is really for you and I will be chucked." Betsy stopped to catch her breath. She looked at me. "So?" she asked.

"So I'm calling him," I offered, "and we're going to just hang out."

As I dialed, Betsy fidgeted on the bed, twitching her quilt and straightening her pillowcases.

"Hey, it's me," I told Jeremy when he answered, "Betsy and I want you to come over for a while, if you want. Everyone else is out, and we can have some ice cream and talk."

He made noncommittal noises into the phone for a minute. I glanced at Betsy and mouthed, "You do it." I tossed her the phone.

When the receiver was against her head, her mouth opened and closed like a dying fish for a few seconds. I didn't share that observation with her. Filtering, once again. Finally she said, "Um, hi, Jeremy." Then there was quiet for a minute, followed by, "I really wish you'd come back." Medium-long pause. Tears. Here we go. "Mmm-hmm. Here's Leigh." She chucked the phone back at me and wiped her juicy nose on her sleeve, making that moment officially the least ladylike one I'd shared with her.

"Hey," I said into the phone.

"I'm coming back."

"I'll roll out the red carpet and break out the lemonade," I replied.

I was scooping ice cream when his car door banged shut. Betsy met my eye, took a deep breath, and went to the door to let him in. I heard them whispering at the door, her sniffling, him murmuring something soothing. Several scoops later, as they made it to the kitchen, they were holding hands. I was glad to see it. No way had they said everything that needed to be said yet, but we (they) had made it over a bump.

⁓

If we wanted to beat the university kids to the good summer jobs, it was time to get moving. I halfheartedly filled out mall applications and sat for interviews. After being home two weeks and getting two job offers (which naturally I had to turn down), I started raising Betsy's suspicions.

"Why are you applying to these places if you don't want to work there?"

"Do I really want to work retail? I guess I'm just holding out for the perfect job. You know, something just right."

She stared at me, making it clear she could see right through my lies. I studied my fingernails.

"Leigh, are you not taking jobs because you think you need to be around for Jeremy? I mean, is there even anything you could do?" Shiny eyes—the tears were near.

What a generous thought. I should grasp on to that one. "Yeah, I guess I'd just feel better if I could always be on call. What if he needs someone?" I knew there was no way I could explain my need to stay close with my eyes locked on him. Like applying pressure in first aid. I was totally unwilling to let my negligence cause him to slip away. When I had gotten distracted in Oklahoma, everything had started to fall apart. And the Trevor thing had been only a few days. What could happen to Jeremy if I was gone full-time?

It was fine with me for Betsy to think that I wanted to be close by to help him. There was no real reason to try to explain that I needed to stay near him for *me*. I had enough guilt issues locked away inside me, and I needed to be certain nothing happened to Jeremy while my attention was diverted. I couldn't bear to be responsible for his body turning on him, attacking him.

"You can't fix him." Betsy stared at the floor while I felt all the blood in my head heat to a boil. Cue my dramatic overreaction.

"What are you saying? That you can? I should go get a job because you want to be the one he calls? You want to be part of the drama? You want to clean up the messes? You want to watch him being so sick he can't sit up? You want to drive him home from treatments?"

"Drive him home? Is that what you think you're going to do? Is that what would finally get you behind the wheel of your car? Do you think you'd drive for him?" Tears were streaming from Betsy's eyes.

"Shut up. You don't know anything about it, so just leave it alone."

"Of course I don't know anything about it. No one will talk about it. My dad won't even tell me what is up with you. You brought it up, so tell me. Why won't you drive your car? Why does it sit out there like a monument, taking up space? It's this huge taboo thing that we all have to look at every day but no one's allowed to mention."

"Even if that was any of your business, I wouldn't talk to you about it. Just try to imagine that there are one or two things in my world that I am not interested in sharing with you." I stomped out of the room and slammed the door.

Chapter 15

Betsy went to Denver for a week at the first of May. Her Grandma Burke needed help after a surgery, and Betsy was the chosen one. It was very okay for me not to be invited. I didn't need to feel any more part of the Burkes. I was, in fact, fairly overwhelmed by the Burkeness of my life. And I could have Jeremy back to myself for a week. She left for the airport loaded up with schoolwork and a pair of huge sunglasses to hide the circles under her eyes.

As she and Paul pulled out of the driveway, I felt the tug— that feeling that there is something important you've forgotten to do (or not forgotten, but neglected, ignored, or turned firmly away from). I grabbed some runners that lay by the door and slammed my feet into them. They were Emily's. Skidding down the front walk, I flagged Paul to stop the car. Lurching with my toes rammed into much-too-small sneakers, I ran to Betsy's window.

Once the car was stopped and the window down, I realized that I had no idea what I wanted to say. Just that there was something I wanted, needed, had to say.

I rested my fingers on Betsy's open window. Looking from

my hand to her sunglasses and back, I waited for inspiration. No such luck.

Finally understanding that I was making as much effort as I possibly could, Betsy reached over, squeezed my hand, and nodded.

"I'm . . ." I tried, but couldn't figure out how to finish.

"Me too," Betsy nodded again.

"Okay. Have a good trip."

"You bet. See you next week. Take good chemistry notes for me."

"Will do. Go safe."

Window rolling up, the car pulled away from the curb. I felt immeasurable relief. I wasn't sure what had just happened, but it seemed like we were going to be okay.

———

Mrs. Bentley let me sit with Jeremy at the second chemo drip appointment. She left us there in the clinic full of all sizes of easy chairs—some disturbingly small. I snuggled into the chair by Jeremy's side and started fussing.

"Do you want a magazine? Your iPod? A movie? What can I get you? Are you thirsty?" Clearly nervous, I turned into my mother for a few minutes.

"Thanks. I don't need anything now. Just talk with me, okay?"

"Sure. Did you know that the Pacific octopus has like 20,000 suckers on its tentacles?"

"Hmm. That's fascinating. Thanks for that. I want to talk about something else."

What could possibly be more captivating than octopus suckers? Oh. Trevor. Sure.

"Okay. So there's this guy. He lives in Oklahoma. That's a state, sort of in the middle. He has some pretty fascinating personality traits. Like Polynesian arms. Have you ever seen real Polynesian arms? That's a thing of beauty. And his hair is longer than yours, but it's curly. And black. And he's just hot, okay?"

"Did you want to kiss him?" This sounded familiar. Maybe I was fated to repeat conversations like this for the rest of my life.

"I did," I smiled.

Jeremy nodded. "Right on. Wait. You did want to? Or you did kiss him?"

"Yes. And yes."

"Good girl. Every day?"

"Not the first two times we went out. You'd be so proud. Not the days I spent hiding under a blanket in Grammy's living room. He steered clear then. Any further questions?"

"Is he good enough for you?"

"He'll do, in a long-distance, never-see-him-again situation. But you might see him. He's going to school up in the mountains with you."

Jeremy nodded to show me he'd heard, but I didn't think he was really paying too much attention. He seemed like he was working up his courage for something. Something other than having poison dripped into his veins.

"You could see him. You never know, Leigh. Life's funny."

"Hmm. Yeah. I'm cracking up here." I looked around the room. A little boy with hair as pale as his very white skin was coloring in a notebook as his mom read him a story. Yeah, life is hilarious.

I decided to let Jeremy lead the conversation for a while. "So, what do you want to talk about?"

"I want you to tell me what happened in the car accident."

Well, *that* came out of nowhere. I sat stunned for a few seconds.

"The car accident? You mean *the* car accident?" I stared at Jeremy's IV. Was he serious? What was the purpose of that? "I've already told you everything. Did you forget some horrible detail that you'd like to revisit? How is this helpful?"

Jeremy shifted in his chair. "I know you're uncomfortable talking about it, but I want you to tell me again. Will you do that for me?" I swear, if he had been a girl, he would have fluttered his lashes right then.

"I don't know. Why do you want to hear it again?"

"I want to know what it felt like."

What it felt like? What did he think it felt like? A day at the beach? It felt horrible. It felt like everything good was gone, never to return. It felt like dark. It felt like too cold, and too hot, and every awful feeling all at once. What it felt like? How do you describe your worst moment? How did he think you're supposed to feel when you kill your dad?

"Leigh, you're the only one I know who's been that close to a dying person. I just want to know if it scared him."

Oh. What it felt like for *him*.

Driving my required forty hours of supervised pre-driver's-license time was an absolute pleasure. Dad let me chauffeur him everywhere. We drove to the university, to Eagle Creek Reservoir, over to the grocery store, and anywhere else we could get to in a car. I could shift out of first gear like a pro. Changing lanes on the freeway was becoming second nature. He taught me to think of SMOG—Signal, Mirrors, Over-the-shoulder, Go! It was dumb, but pretty effective.

Then the pleasure turned to nightmare.

If you haven't seen autumn in Indiana, you've missed one of the greatest earthly pleasures. Red, orange, and green don't even begin to describe it. Ten minutes in any direction out of the city you can pull onto a back road and find a canopy of trees over the road. There are houses, but you can't see them tucked away there. Just trees, wind, birds, and the thoughts in your head.

Dad and I were out on a road like that. I was always cautious on those drives, because the roads weren't quite wide enough for two cars at any kind of speed. But, Dad insisted, driving faster actually made the cars thinner so they could pass easier. One of Newton's more neglected laws of physics, apparently.

Disregarding Newton's Lost Law of Automotive Skinniness, I kept the speed low.

The road curved to the left.

We curved to the left.

Laughing about Newton, we curved along the road to the right.

He put his hand on the back of my head.

He told me what a great driver I was becoming.

A blue jay shrieked above us and we both looked up.

Then we were jolting to the left—hard.

Something heavy hit my shoulder. Dad's head.

Glass was shattering, mixing its terrifying music with the birdsong.

My head bashed into my window frame and I heard screaming.

It was me.

⁓

The driver of the blue Camaro had taken his hidden driveway at a run, and we were in exactly the right place at the wrong time. If I had gone faster, like Dad had suggested, we'd have been long gone before he zoomed out of his driveway. If I had closed the windows, I wouldn't have been looking at that blue jay. If I hadn't been the driver, Dad wouldn't have been in that passenger's seat. If I had been able to brake more smoothly, his head wouldn't have thumped the dash that last time.

I would never drive again.

⁓

"Germ, of all the things I have to feel bad about, all the things I wish I could erase, at least I don't worry about him suffering. He didn't have time to be scared. He didn't see it coming, and he . . . he didn't last long enough to wonder what had happened."

"Will you just tell me? Whatever you can remember. Please? I just want to know."

Staring at the arm of his chair, I told him everything. All of it. Each detail scratched into my brain and heart. The story I held, untold, in my secret place. The warm wind suddenly growing cooler as we entered the tree tunnels. The gentle pressure of Dad's hand on my head, and then his arm flying past my shoulder toward the driver's side window. The scrape of metal and screeching tires echoing the birds' songs. The sickening, sweet smell of blood swamping the car as my brain spun to remember which was the brake pedal. The remarkable and frightening calm with which I reached into my dead father's shirt pocket for the cell phone.

"Then there's the next hour or so, which for all I remember may never have happened. The EMTs had to untangle my fingers from my dad's mangled hand. His hand had been pushed into the frame beside me on impact. I tried to straighten out his fingers, I guess. Then I just sat there holding his hand until they made me move so they could pull him out of the driver's door. My legs were like jelly and someone sat me at the side of the road. I really wanted to throw up, but, you know—I could never do that in front of people. So I watched the emergency crew drag Dad's body out over the gearshift and across the seat.

"The passenger side of the car was smooshed like an accordion and the front windshield had buckled. Camaro Guy was having mild hysterics and the EMTs were mopping blood out of his eyes. He had a pretty good gash on his forehead—you know how head cuts bleed. His car was thrashed, but he was okay. And I had a bump on the side of my head, a cut-up knee, and a sprained shoulder where Dad's head landed just after I broke his neck." I was feeling hot and flushy and I knew I needed very badly to cry, but this was not a place for a scene.

Staring at the arm of Jeremy's chair, I whispered, "I didn't mean to hurt him. I had no idea that I could make something that horrible happen. Who thinks about that kind of possibility when they start a car? But since it's obviously a thing I can't control, I can't drive. I won't take other people's fate into my hands again. There are already too many things out there that can hurt us. I don't need to be one of those things."

Looking over at Jeremy at last, I saw tears flowing from his eyes. He reached over and took my hand in both of his. He closed his eyes, but tears still leaked out from under his eyelids, and the crying policy went into immediate effect. My tears came too—not in an elegant and ladylike manner, but in waves and gasps. I buried my head in his shoulder and sobbed. A nurse hurried over with tissues and, bless her beautiful heart, said nothing. She simply brought another blanket like Jeremy's and tucked me in. We sat there like that, him holding my hand over his heart, my arms tangled in his chemo drip, saying nothing and crying till we were dry.

Long minutes later, I heard, "What happened to your dad was not your fault. You didn't hurt him. You were the victim of an accident. *Accident,* as in *not your fault.* Not. Your. Fault." There was a sniffle-filled pause. "Tomorrow," Germ finally whispered, "we start driving lessons."

And so, beginning as slowly and gently as he knew how, Jeremy taught me to drive. On the first day, we sat in the Jeep parked in the garage. He had me go through each of the gears, dry-shifting with the clutch in and the motor off. After a relaxing lunch of canned ravioli and a game of Scrabble (in which I kicked Jeremy's chicken), we actually pulled the keys off the hook by the door and put them in the ignition.

The second day, we opened the garage door and started the car. We pulled the Jeep out of the garage and backed out of the driveway. Seeing my face turning purple from me holding my breath, he called it good and drove back in for me.

I'm not sure driving is a skill you can lose by not practicing, but confidence is.

Day by day, with my best friend at my side, I regained my confidence.

After a few drives where we actually left not only the driveway but the entire neighborhood, Jeremy and I came in one day to find a postcard from Grammy on the table. It had a bizarre photo of a chimp wearing a purple tutu (well, why not?).

> Dear Leigh and Betsy, darlings,
> Blood is thicker than water, yes. But remember—a good smoothie is thicker than either (and much tastier) and that's what we've got between us.
> Hugs and kisses,
> Grammy

Jeremy smiled after I showed him the postcard. "She's good, your Grammy. Such a gift with words."

"To be so endowed, yeah? You don't need her words, though. You're a magician. You've managed to get Betsy and me to sort of tolerate each other in your own mysterious way. I guess I'm glad you've been here between us. A safety buffer, you know, so we didn't kill each other." I nudged him with my elbow.

"You didn't need me. You guys would have become great friends without me. But I'm glad I've been here, too. Where else can a guy see action like in this house? This is the best show in town, kind of like a tennis match with everything going back and forth."

For the first time I recognized that not only might we have become friends without Jeremy, but we might have become even better friends if he hadn't been around. He *was* a safety buffer between us, but no matter how you looked at it, he was still between us. Just like Betsy was now between Jeremy and me, and I managed to be between the two of them. It was so tangled up and . . . triangular.

"Do you miss her yet?" we both asked. I gave a noncommittal shrug. I would not be the first to admit to anything.

Jeremy smiled. "It's been great to have you to myself this week. I'm not that good at sharing you. It's kind of hard not to be jealous of Betsy, because she gets you all the time. I'm glad we've had time just to be ourselves again. But even being alone together, we're different, don't you think? You're different than you used to be. Maybe your fling made you sweeter. I should thank that guy."

Rolling my eyes, I silently denied any sweetness on my part.

"And I'm definitely different. Don't you find me more charming? More chivalrous? More exciting and dashing and, um . . . tall?"

"Absolutely tall. You haven't changed, though. You're still the same Germ I haven't been able to shake since seventh grade." I faked a sneeze.

"Bless you, you little rat." He bumped the back of my

knees and I collapsed onto the floor. Leaping to my side, he pinned my shoulders to the kitchen tile with his elbows. I squirmed around enough to give him a fight. He reached my face with his hands, holding me still.

I felt my stomach lurch in an unaccustomed way. Jeremy laughed his victory, but quickly became serious as he looked down at me. In all these years of playing around and being crazy and being calm together, I'd never seen quite that look in his face. Tender, accepting, and a little sad, I honestly had a moment where I thought he was going to kiss me. Like a real kiss. There was something in that look that reminded me of Trevor. He brushed a runaway hair off my cheek. I bit my bottom lip. He was still sprawled on the floor beside me on his elbows. My breath came more quickly than usual, and I tried to think Yogic thoughts. Jeremy brought his face closer.

Whispering, with his nose almost touching mine, he said, "This is it."

This is it? *This is it?* This is what? This is the beginning of the end? This is the assassination of the Archduke Franz Ferdinand that will bring about the World War in the Burke/Mason family? The moment everything I thought I knew turns out to be an enormous mistake? I wanted to tell him that this was really *not* it. That as much as I loved him, there was no reason to ruin all kinds of lives.

"This is what I want to live for," he whispered.

Years of memories suddenly filled my head. School memories, home memories, play, work, study. Jeremy and I playing basketball, Jeremy and I riding the bus. Jeremy and I talking on the phone. Jeremy and I grieving together. Jeremy and I talking about girls, about boys, about the deep meanings of the universe. Bike rides. Ice cream at his house. Scones at my house. Gallons of lemonade, hours of laughing. Suddenly I understood. Friendship like we had did make it all worthwhile. I reached up to touch his arm.

"I want you to live for it, too. We'll get you well. And whatever's coming next will be better than ever."

"You are my best friend, Leigh. I love you. I adore you. I treasure you. You make me strong." Pulling me to sit up, he wrapped me up in his arms. "I'm fighting this and I'm going to beat it. You will help me, right? You'll be here with me to keep me strong?"

Pulling back so I could look straight into his face, I promised to do whatever he needed.

He leaned over and gently, softly kissed my cheek. "Go, team," he whispered.

Chapter 16

Betsy's return from Denver brought the strangest web of emotions. Sarah and Emily could barely contain their bodily fluids, they were so excited. Paul's relief to have her back was as obvious as you'd expect, seeing as he lived in a house very full of other people's daughters. Now at least he could count on understanding (to some extent) one family member's mood shifts. Mom was all smiles, as usual these days.

And me? Strangely enough, I was nervous for her to come back. But not in the something-I've-been-dreading way; more like in the I-really-want-you-to-be-comfortable way. Like that first date feeling. I wanted her to *want* to come home—and for this to be home. Until the day she returned, I hadn't really admitted how I missed her. I was too busy trying to learn (again) to drive. But she needed to know that I really had missed her. If there was any lingering doubt that I liked her in my family, I wanted to erase it now.

Totally aware how out of character it seemed, as soon as I saw Betsy round the corner toward the bag claim, I ran to her and squished her into a serious sister hug.

"Good trip?" I asked.

"Pretty good. I guess if I had to choose between cooking for, cleaning up after, and generally entertaining a grandma who sits up in her adjustable bed all day watching *The Price Is Right* versus going out for pedicures and smoothies, I'd have to pick your Grammy any day. But Grandma Burke needed me, and off to the rescue I went, ta-da. Not much fun, but we do what we have to do for the people we love." She smiled and shrugged.

The baggage carriage started to whine, and as I watched the metal hinges mesh around the turn, her words echoed in my head. *We do what we have to do for the people we love.*

Guilt settled like a large, hot rock in my stomach. What had I done for anyone lately? Each of my actions over the past several months fitted nicely into one category—Whatever Makes Me Feel Better. Standing beside Betsy, who tried to smooth over every lump in our family situation, who tiptoed around with her boyfriend because he happened to also be my best friend, who voluntarily left pleasant situations for unpleasant ones, I felt like an ogre. *Selfish* didn't even begin to describe me. I was, as my dad would have said, a blockhead. Not only was I not helping, I was hurting everyone I loved.

I was, consciously or not, turning the twins away from Betsy, and, by extension, from Paul. Jeremy suffered guilt on every occasion of every day, thanks to me. I must have broken his heart right in half—one side for her, one for me—by making him choose, when what was there to choose? I could still be his best friend if he had a girlfriend. Sure, it would be different. But was having him all to myself the only way I could feel wanted? Could Mom and Paul possibly be as happy as they deserved to be, knowing that their marriage had turned a fairly normal girl into a snarling, sarcastic beast? What would Grammy have thought if she'd known how I really felt about Betsy sometimes? She'd have been ashamed of me for withholding my kindness, friendship, and even basic consideration.

What would Dad have done? I had pushed this thought away so many times, because it was counterintuitive. If he'd been here, none of this would be happening. Somehow—subconsciously, I hope—I had reversed cause and effect by making Betsy and Paul the reason Dad was gone. As though he might come back if they disappeared. As ridiculous as it sounds, I was holding out my affection in case it prevented Dad's return.

Now I forced myself to consider what he would have done. Staring at the turning baggage carriage, I realized how ashamed of me he would have been. The last person in the world to withhold affection from anyone, he'd have been appalled to see how I'd handled the Great Experiment. He would have welcomed new family (even replacement family) with charm and grace that would have made them feel a seamless part of the group. He would have received a new person into his heart and done whatever it took to expand his definition of family.

With the deepest breath I could readily grasp, I raised my arm to Betsy's shoulders. "I missed you. I'm glad you're back. I'm glad you're home."

Squeezing me around the waist, Betsy smiled, "I'm glad to be home too."

"I have a little surprise for you. I made Jeremy promise not to tell while you were gone."

"He did mention that the two of you were working on

something, but he wouldn't say what." She looked confused—
maybe as much at the pending surprise as at my recent displays of affection.

"There's your bag. Let's go." I grabbed her suitcase and
wheeled it out to the curb, where Jeremy was waiting in my
Jeep.

He jumped out of the driver's seat and hugged Betsy. Putting the suitcase in the back, I ignored whatever else might be
happening between them over there in the loading/unloading
zone and jumped in behind the wheel. Jeremy climbed in
behind me as Betsy stared openmouthed at me.

"Come on, buckle up. Nobody rides in my car unpro-
tected," I smiled. Taking a deep breath, I pushed in the clutch
and started the engine. We headed home.

———

Weeks passed in this new routine of comfortable disarray.
School, homework, treatments, outings. When Jeremy's hair
thinned to the point where anyone would notice, he came over
for The Shaving. Betsy had already officially lost her sense of
humor about chemotherapy and all that it implied, but Germ
gave it his best shot to create a comedy, insisting on a full-scale
video production complete with fog machines and strobe
lights.

I pulled the Jeep out into the driveway and created a
makeshift movie set in the garage. After old sheets were
draped against walls and lights were rigged, we pulled the haircut kit out of the linen closet and set to work. Paul ran the
camera, the twins gave a rather impressive drumroll on a

bucket, and Betsy and I took turns buzzing off Jeremy's remaining hair. His running commentary had us all in hysterics, and we were wiping juicy eyes and noses as we went along "assisting the chemo" into Full Bentley Baldness.

When the hair was gone and Mom had touched up the totally atrocious job we'd done, we all trooped into the kitchen to make cookies. Huddled into a chair at the edge of the room, Betsy continued to wipe her eyes long after the rest of us had stopped. Let's not sugarcoat it, she was a wreck. Germ, holding court for the twins, didn't seem to notice. Letting my better urges win out for once, I quietly made my way over to her chair. Handing her a tissue, I put my arm over her shoulders and rested my head on hers. For several minutes we stayed like that, watching the rest of our family play with our favorite guy. They were all having such a normal, great time.

"It's kind of horrible, isn't it?" Betsy finally whispered.

I let out a quiet laugh. "Which part?"

Smiling, she said, "All of it, but mainly the hair."

"Yeah, but he's got a great-shaped head. It could be worse if he were one of those lumpy guys. And he's good-looking enough to pull it off."

Jeremy must have finally felt us watching him, because he turned and looked at us. Gracing us with the most fantastic of his smiles, he threw a wink. Emily immediately swiped his nose with the gooey spatula, and he returned to the task at hand.

Betsy and I smiled and in perfect unison whispered, "We're so lucky."

Laughing in surprise, Betsy pulled me into the chair, gave me a quick hug, and then dumped me on the floor. Leaping over me, she lunged across the kitchen to Sarah—just in time to intercept the taste of cookie dough on her finger. Mom and Paul laughed.

If anyone had been looking through the windows (and thank goodness no one was), we would have looked just like a family.

Later that evening, while Betsy was showering, Mom came in and flopped down on my bed. "Hey, kiddo. How we doing?"

I stretched and repositioned so she could play with my hair. She had perfect nails for head-scratches. "What a crazy day. I'm wiped out."

"We've got to get your Jeremy out in the sun. That bald-head look needs a little help," she smiled. She brushed the hair out of my eyes and gave me a classic Mom look, like she was studying me so she couldn't forget what she was seeing. My favorite thing about getting a gaze like that from her was that she had approval written all over her. She could only see what I was doing right. I hadn't felt a look like that for a while. Months, in fact.

"My Leigh. I wanted to come in here while you were alone, because I want to tell you something." She smiled peacefully and I felt a wave of dread and nausea wash over me.

"You're not pregnant, are you?" I gasped, sitting up and pulling my hair from her fingers.

She laughed, surprised. "No. Not even close. But if I had been, you could have responded more gracefully, I think. No, this is not an announcement. But you know what? That was a classic face, and my heart took a picture of you just now," she laughed. "No, I just need to thank you for something. I can tell you now that tonight made a whole bunch of other nights worthwhile. You did good today."

"What do you mean?"

Taking a deep breath, she leaned up on one elbow, facing me on the bed. Her other hand stroked my hair as she hunted for gentle words. "I know that life has not turned out the way we planned. I realize that this family transition has been tough on you. I understand that your little world has been shaken up and turned upside down. But I don't know if you understand how your feelings and especially your actions and words reflect on the rest of us.

"Anyone with a heart like yours and a mind like yours and a personality like yours is going to get noticed. You have been the emotional barometer of our family for years. I could always count on you for comedy, for fun, for good feelings. You're like our household sunshine. We could always count on your attitude to rub off on the family; but, babe, it goes both ways.

"When you feel great, we feel it. But when you're miserable, nobody can avoid that, either. There has been a tangible dark cloud over our home for months, and none of us has been able to find the sunshine like we want to. But today, wow. I think every one of us could tell that there was a difference. Thanks for bringing back the light."

Tears started leaking out of my eyes. I felt applauded and condemned at the same time. Why was she being so kind? I didn't deserve it, because apparently I'd been the bad guy. This was all news to me. I had no idea that my heartache was casting a shadow big enough to touch my whole household—my whole family. This was supposed to be between Betsy and me, and, in my nastiness, I hadn't particularly cared if I hurt her.

But I'd honestly had no idea that I had been making Mom feel bad. That was never the plan. Being so wrapped up inside my drama-queen role of Suffering Adolescent, I hadn't even considered how my attitude affected anyone else in our home.

"I didn't know any of that. Do you believe me?" I sniffled.

"Leigh, in so many ways you are wise beyond your years, but I have never forgotten that you are really still a kid. My kid. My baby, my little princess, my joy and delight. I didn't come in here to tell you you've been doing everything wrong. But without knowing what you've been causing around here, you would never be able to appreciate how grateful and thrilled I am tonight. You did a great thing. You gave everyone the permission you've been holding back: permission to behave like a family. And it makes me really happy."

"I'm sorry, Mom. I'll try . . . you know."

"I know. You'll do great. We'll be fine. Maybe not a quick and easy Happily Ever After, but we'll get there. All of us together."

~

As we rocketed forward toward the end of the school year, Jeremy's side effects got more severe. He was weakening quickly enough so that even I noticed—I, who would have been capable of ignoring striped horns growing out of his head if it meant I didn't have to think about him being hurt, being sick, feeling awful, fighting pain, fighting death. There. I acknowledged it. Jeremy could very well be dying. Dying. Of all the ways I was likely to lose him, this should have been the most obvious, but I'd managed to block it from my mind.

Because of all the ways to lose him, this was the permanent one. The most horribly unfixable one.

Across the board, teachers made finals easy for him. They allowed him to take tests early, to finish assignments before the rest of us, to skip all the unimportant parts. Lying on my back on his bedroom floor with my feet up on the bed, I quizzed him for exams while Betsy sat beside him, holding his hand, scratching his back, wiping her tears. She seemed to never run dry. But she couldn't stay away from him any more than I could.

He finished all his requisites and performed beautifully on his exams. Just in time, as it happened. Three days before graduation, Jeremy was admitted to the hospital. We weren't able to see him the first two days, and Betsy and I were on the phone to the nurses' station fairly constantly for information and updates. We had a favorite nurse, Wendy, who gave out much better information than any of the others. She'd tell us if he was awake or asleep, how long he'd been out of his room, how many family members were stalking the hallways, all the goods.

Friday morning after our last exam we jumped into the Jeep and made our first appearance in the ward. The nurses at the desk smiled at us and pointed out Jeremy's door without our having to ask.

"Who's Wendy?" Betsy asked. A large woman with curly gray hair was coming around the desk.

She squeezed us together and said, "You're Betsy. And you're Leigh. I'm so happy to finally meet you," as though she'd been hearing about us for years, not two days.

As we walked into his room, Jeremy was just hanging up the phone.

"Hey, it's my two favorite ladies. How were the exams?" His voice was raspy and scratchy—like his throat had been rubbed raw. Huge purple circles sat below his eyes, but his grin was perfect, as always. Betsy and I each pulled up a chair, one on either side of the bed. At the same time we leaned over and each kissed a cheek.

With a quiet laugh, Jeremy whispered, "Now, that's what I'm talking about. Not just anybody gets this kind of treatment. You two have just made this all worth it." His smile almost hid the little grimace in his eyes.

"You hurting?" I asked.

"Not anymore. You two are better than morphine." He reached out and took each of us by a hand. With a deep breath that was almost a sigh, he settled into the pillows.

"Mr. Kingston called just before you came. He heard there was no way I could make it to graduation. He asked who I wanted to pick up my diploma." Jeremy paused and looked at each of us in turn. "I told him I wanted my mom to do it. Is that okay?"

"Perfect," Betsy jumped in. "Exactly right."

Ah, Jeremy. Always the diplomat. The only person I knew who could think of absolutely everyone but himself. "So, come on," he asked, giving our hands a squeeze, "how did the exams go?"

Chapter 17

Graduation day dawned muggy and overcast. As Betsy and I got ready to go, I felt yucky. "Can't we skip it?" I whined as I brushed blush onto my face. "Who's going to notice if we're not there?"

"You mean besides our parents, the twins, and the rest of the graduating class?"

"Yeah, besides them," I smiled. "You look gorgeous. I can't believe you even make a cap and gown ensemble look hot. Completely unfair, you know."

"Please, Leigh. Look at us both. We are fabulous. Grammy would be delighted. But we should have done our toes. Then she'd really be pleased."

Laughing, we walked out into the kitchen. Two large rectangular boxes lay on the table. Inside each were a dozen pink roses tied with a ribbon. Betsy's name was on the one tied in yellow—her color of happiness and contentment. The card attached read: *"Betsy, sweet, I couldn't find anything to fit your triceps. Please accept this bracelet and, for today, love your wrist. Big kisses, Grammy."*

My roses were tied in blue. Bright, shocking blue, like my

Oklahoma pedicure. *"My Leigh, your miracle is happening. You're making it so. Please pull your hair back so everyone can see these divine earrings dangling from your perfect ears. All my love and a half, Grammy."* A tiny jewelry box rested in the blue ribbon. Inside were seriously gorgeous sapphire earrings in the same shade of miraculous bright blue. Betsy and I helped each other into our new jewels and walked to the mirror hanging over the fireplace. Standing there side by side, we glanced from our own faces to each other's, and for just a minute, I could see Grammy's bright blue miracle flit between us.

Taking a deep breath, I squeezed Betsy's waist. "Let's do this thing."

The parking lot was more than half full when we pulled the Jeep in. Mom, Paul, and the twins would follow. We jumped out, straightened our flowing polyester grad gowns, and headed for the auditorium. The seats at the front had little numbers taped to them so we could know just where to sit. Alphabetically, natch. Matching names to numbers was the enviable job of Mr. Kingston, school counselor extraordinaire and graduation point man. So Betsy found her spot near the front, as I hid (whether I wanted to or not) smack in the middle.

After a short rehearsal, the orchestra tuned up and the curtain was closed. Families gathered in the auditorium seats as I fidgeted among my classmates, many of whom I wouldn't see much after this event. I tried to care. For a few short moments I watched people like Penny Goldman blot tears and hug friends, but I couldn't help feeling apart. Why? Wasn't I attached to these people? Didn't it mean anything to me that we'd spent years entrenched in the public school system together? Was I incapable of connecting myself to them? Wasn't it kind of sick that I may never see them again and I didn't really care? Maybe that piece of my heart devoted to making friends and learning to love people was calloused. Scarred over.

Then, from the front of the auditorium, Betsy turned and caught my eye. She grinned and gave a little wave of her bracelet. I smiled and waggled my head so my earrings shimmied. There was room in my heart for Betsy. I managed to like her (not that it was such a chore—she was probably the most likable female anywhere) when I didn't care too much about the majority of high school girls. Maybe my scarred heart wasn't shut off, just selective. She faked flicking tears off her cheeks and rolled her beautiful eyes. We shared a silent laugh as the curtain opened.

Prayers, songs, and speeches carried on just long enough to cause me to wonder why they made us sit through this. Then Mr. Kingston announced the processional, and the orchestra began what I knew would be innumerable repetitions of "Pomp and Whatever It's Called." Just as the last of the A people filed back into their seats to make way for the Bs, I saw Jeremy's mom walk past our row and up the stairs. She waited patiently on the corner of the stage while Jeff Beatty (no relation to Warren), Chandra Beckstead, and Maddie Beeson received their diplomas and cursory administrative handshakes. Suddenly a projected image about 25 feet tall appeared on the screen behind the podium. Mr. Kingston paused as he turned to look at the enormous and handsome Jeremy-face blasted on the wall.

"Accepting a diploma on behalf of Jeremy Bentley, his mother, Michelle."

A moment of nearly total silence followed as Mrs. Bentley made her way to the middle of the stage. Then, almost as one, the entire senior class was on its feet. Cheering, stamping, whistling, and whooping just about blew Mrs. Bentley off the stage. She staggered a little, then stood steady, looking into the faces of the cheering mob. A lovely and peaceful smile grew on her face as tears spilled down her cheeks. I felt her eyes seeking me out, and when we connected, she blew me a kiss.

She held up Jeremy's diploma, turned to look at the gigantic photo of her son, and raised her hand in a small wave before she walked back down the stairs to her seat. The cheering continued, on and on, until I realized the person who needed most to hear it was miles away. I pulled my phone out and speed-dialed Jeremy's cell. He picked up on the first ring, and I held the phone up to transmit all that love.

"Hear that? That's all for you, and now I have to go before I get busted. Be good."

"Thanks, Leigh. You're the best. Love you. 'Bye."

Now why was I crying? I felt a huge urge to reach out and hug anyone within my reach. I wanted to wrap the entire senior class up and put them in my pocket. Who was I kidding that I wasn't attached to these people? Anyone who loved my Germ that much had to be excellent. Such good taste had to come from fathomless wells of kindness. I felt closer to this group than I ever had as we shared those few minutes of celebration for Jeremy.

As soon as it was decent to escape, meaning after the requisite family photos, Betsy and I bowed out of the post-grad festivities and headed back to the hospital. Rain was pounding, and the wipers were flying across the windshield. As we crossed town with the streets running like little rivers, Betsy was thoughtful.

"What are you thinking about?" I asked her.

There was a long pause. Maybe she didn't want to tell me. That was fine, even if it was more characteristic of me than of her. I stole a glance at her while I checked my rearview mirror.

"If Jeremy doesn't make it, will we be okay?"

I slammed the brake down to the floor, locking my elbows against the steering wheel. Betsy's arm flew out to the dash, bracing her. Even the Jeep's super-traction tires had a hard time with that maneuver.

"Do not ever, ever say those words again," I hissed. My head was pounding with rage and terror. Cars rushed past us sending fans of water onto the side of the Jeep, and I realized that I needed to get off the road. Or at least out of the lane.

"Leigh, I just meant . . ." Betsy tried to swallow the awful thing she had just said.

"Stop. Just shut up. Don't say a word." I felt dangerous. Stalling twice in first gear, I finally got my head around getting the car moving. I turned off into a gas station and parked by the empty car wash. The rain battered the hood and glass. Looking down at my hands, I saw that my knuckles were white. Veins in the backs of my hands stood out, pulsing with my fury. Staring at the steering wheel, I began a rant that had been building for weeks.

"Now you listen to me, Betsy. There is no question of

anyone not making it. Jeremy will get well. He has to. If you're
not willing to practice a little positive thinking here, then you
should not be coming. Just take your stupid doubts and go
home."

I half hoped and half feared that she would actually get out
of the car and walk home in the rain.

"You're not up for this, you've said so yourself. So get out
of the way and let me handle it. I know what's going on here. I
know what Jeremy wants, and I know what he needs. He
needs support. He needs strength. He needs ice cream and
lemonade. He needs bravery and good attitudes. He needs . . ."

"He needs us," she whispered.

"No. He needs *me*."

Betsy did a little shocked gasp that sounded like I'd
punched her in the stomach. It seemed like I'd punched
myself, if that was possible. Could that have been the most
completely selfish thing I'd ever said? It was sure up there on
the list. I felt sick. My heart was thrashed, torn between anger
and remorse and humiliation and regret. I didn't dare to look
at Betsy, to see the hurt I'd just caused. I stared at my wrists
and wished I could take it all back. It was so cruel. So ugly. So
wrong.

"You're right," she said. Her voice was soft, but steady.

I looked right into her lovely face and saw that she wasn't
crying.

How could she not be crying now? She probably cried
when she stepped on an ant. Anything could set her off. Why
wasn't she crying now that there was something really worth
crying about?

And what did she mean, I was right?

"What do you mean?" Well, I just had to know.

"You're right. It's you that Jeremy needs now. You are the one who has pulled him through all the other times. You understand this. You know what to say, what to do, how to make him laugh. You know the drills. You are the one he depends on. You are his favorite person, and he needs you now. But Leigh, he wants me, too."

Why did that hurt so much?

"As much as I want him to have what he needs, can't you let him have what he wants?" Her voice was starting to shake. I knew her tears were coming, and mine were right behind.

Why couldn't I just say it? Why couldn't I just admit to her that I didn't want to share? If I stepped aside now, when it could be the end, my Jeremy could disappear while he held onto someone else's hand. But no. We couldn't talk about that because I had forbidden any discussion of worst-case scenarios.

But I could not deny that she had a point. He did want her there. He wanted both of us. And a strange understanding was dawning on me, slowly and probably very late. Jeremy wanted us there together because Betsy and I just might need each other more than ever very soon. He understood that he might not leave the hospital. And that Betsy and I had to have some-thing to lean on. Something like a friend.

"I'm sorry I'm such a jerk," I whimpered.

Betsy took my hands and squeezed them in hers. "You are a tremendous person of character and depth. You have shared things and people no one could have expected you to share. You have opened new rooms in your heart and made a place for me. I owe you every kind of thanks. You have given me the one thing I always wanted and learned never to hope for."

What had I given her that she could possibly have wanted? No one would have ever hoped for the grief I'd given. Nobody could have wished for the constant sense of unwelcome. I looked at her in confusion. Clearly I had no idea what that one thing was.

Smiling, Betsy brought my hands to her face and kissed my palms. "You gave me a sister."

Chapter 18

Pulling into the hospital's parking garage, Betsy and I attempted to redeem ourselves in the mirror. Yikes. Scary residue of emotional females. Puffy eyes, swollen noses, tracks of makeup, and sniffles. We did the best we could to hide the traces of our breakdown. The nurses at the desk smiled and waved as we passed. We knocked on the closed door and waited. Jeremy's mom opened the door and invited us to join their graduation party.

Balloons, streamers, cake, music, and the Bentley family filled the little room. In the windowsill beside a framed photo of Betsy and me in the Children's Museum was Jeremy's diploma. Glancing over at the bed, I saw how pleased he looked. He had a graduation cap perched on his shiny head and was drinking something out of a hospital jug. Lemonade, natch. Betsy and I waved and tried to blend into the walls until the fiesta wrapped up. His older siblings and their families came around, taking turns to make small talk with Betsy and me. Betsy held a small girl on her lap until the little person fell asleep. It felt like we had a few minutes with everyone in the room except for Jeremy.

As the Bentleys left for the evening, I thanked them for letting us join their party. Mrs. Bentley gave me that gorgeous
smile and hugged us. "Drive carefully if you're going around to
parties, girls," she needlessly cautioned us.

We assured her we'd be safe, and as the group filed out I felt
myself relax. Not that I didn't love Jeremy's family, but I experienced that obvious relief at finding myself with the people I really
wanted to be with. Betsy and I perched on chairs on either side
of Jeremy's bed. Now that the family was gone, he looked tired.

"How do you feel? Do you need anything?" Betsy asked.

"I'm good, thanks. A little wiped out, but good. Happy." He
took each of us by the hand. "So, how was your day?" He
grinned.

"Excellent. But we missed you. Well, Leigh and I did. I
don't think anyone else noticed that you weren't there," Betsy
shrugged.

I gasped. "What have I done? Since when are you sarcastic? I've . . . I've ruined you!" I feigned emotional trauma as
Jeremy laughed.

"I guess it's a latent family trait rising to the surface after all
this time," Betsy smiled at me. "Hey, check out our new spark-
lies." She waved her wrist at Jeremy and pointed out my earrings.

"Ooh, very nice. That reminds me. I have something for
you guys. Behind your picture, can you see it?" There was a
small wrapped box sitting on the windowsill. I reached for it
and handed it to Betsy to open. She took care not to tear the
ribbon or paper and slowly and gently removed the lid. Inside
were two silver chains. She picked one up and handed it over
to me. I held it up and saw that the pendant was a perfect silver triangle. Hers was identical.

Jeremy smiled. "Do you like them?" he asked, almost shyly. "It's us, see? Our little love triangle."

Betsy and I leaned across the bed to help each other fasten on the necklaces. "Beautiful," I said, and Betsy smiled at me. Then we both leaned down and kissed Jeremy's head. Sliding back into the chairs, we got comfy to talk over the day.

After a couple of hours, we could see Jeremy was exhausted. "We'd better go now," I whispered as his eyes started to close again.

"Mmm. Sorry. Please stay a little longer. I mean, unless you have somewhere else to be?"

We all agreed that there was no place we'd rather spend this evening.

I opened my eyes when I heard a beeping over my head. My neck felt like it was in a vise clamp. And I was drooling. Lovely. I raised my head slowly so I wouldn't disturb Jeremy, and saw him sleeping peacefully, his color much better now. Betsy's gorgeous hair was tousled on Jeremy's other shoulder. He was still holding each of our hands, and somehow during our snooze, Betsy and I had connected, too. My left arm was twined into Jeremy's IV tube, and my right was resting across his stomach, holding Betsy's hand.

I looked at her perfectly tapered fingers, her beautiful skin tone, her fabulous hair. For the first time I didn't feel jealous. I didn't want to be her. I wanted her to be her. I wanted Germ to be Germ (but maybe with hair) and I wanted to be me. Just me, here connected with the two people who would always love me and forgive me. The two people who understood me, laughed with me, and cared about me. My two best friends.

Epilogue

"Leigh! Hustle! We're going to be late!" Emily called from the doorway. She was becoming so bossy. How cute.

I grabbed my camera and pulled a sweater off the hook. Running into Emily, I said, "Come on, what are you waiting for? We're going to be late."

She put her tongue out and I laughed. We grabbed our coats and jumped into the minivan. It was Paul's gift to Mom this Christmas. A nice gesture, really, but we'd only need it when we were all together. It smelled new and clean. Sarah and Betsy were buckled into the backseat.

"Mom, do we have all the presents?" I asked.

"Everything that was left under the tree is here," she assured me.

Paul backed out of the driveway and headed the car toward the Bentleys' house. I was jumpy and antsy in my chair. After first semester finals, Betsy and I had come right home. Home to our shared room and no responsibilities for two whole weeks. Home to days of taking walks in the snow and nights of staying up way too late talking. Home to no Jeremy.

His family had gone to Utah for the usual grandparent visit

and just gotten in last night. We were all having Christmas dinner together. Besides the stack of Bentley gifts, there was a gorgeous brownie trifle packed in the van.

Betsy and I were both nervous as we stood on the front porch, arms full of gifts. She reached over and squeezed my hand. I squeezed back and gave what I hoped was a bracing smile.

Jeremy's mom opened the door. She welcomed us inside. Betsy and I each got a hug and a kiss on the cheek, and she ushered us into the dining room. Mr. Bentley was there cutting into the biggest turkey I'd ever seen. A couple of Jeremy's brothers stood near the door while sisters fussed over the food. The nieces and nephews were running around, so Sarah and Emily made themselves at home. I turned to ask Mrs. Bentley how I could help, and there he was.

He was carrying a crystal pitcher of water in from the kitchen. I walked over to him, took the pitcher, and set it on the serving table, leaving his hands free to catch Betsy as she leaped at him from behind me. I straightened the pitcher while they had their hello, then went over for my turn.

"Welcome home, Germ," I said, as he lifted me off the floor. He kissed my cheek and held me tight.

"I've missed you," he said. "It's great to have you here."

"You need a haircut," I teased.

"Oh, forget it. I have worked so hard for this hair. It's staying," he said.

Reaching out for Betsy with his free arm, he held onto us both. "You two look great. I want to hear all about school. I want to hear over again all the stories you've already told me. I want to hear about what you've been doing without me for two whole weeks. And then, if you're interested, I'll tell you that I met someone."

Betsy stiffened and looked shocked.

"Someone," Jeremy continued, "with black curls and huge arms. And I am secure enough to tell you that he's very good-looking." I could see Betsy relax and grin at me. Suddenly all my nerve endings were on high alert. I could feel the tips of my hair. "When he heard me talking to a friend about Indianapolis, he came running over to me and asked me if I knew a girl named Leigh. I said I'd never heard of her, of course." I pretended to slap him. "Then he came up and saw you two plastered all over the walls of my room, and I couldn't get him out. I think he's still there, staring at your pictures."

He pulled a wrapped gift off a side table and handed it to me. I looked at him, questioning. He shrugged and told me to open it. There was a little card, a folded-up piece of paper, really, that said, "When I think about you I get all warm inside. Merry Christmas from Trevor." I had to indulge in one big shiver. The gift was wrapped in one of those shimmery fabric bags, like what wine comes in. I was pretty sure Trevor wasn't sending me wine, though. Untying the strings slowly, savoring the anticipation for all four seconds that I could stand it, I slid the bottle out of the bag.

Crazy Eddie's XXX Fire-Breathing Hot Sauce. In a handy 12.5-ounce bottle.

"Wow. That's really, um. . . . Okay. That's just weird," Betsy said. "Why couldn't he have sent a huge, blown-up poster of his face? That would have been a good gift."

"Yeah, it would. But this is special. This I can share with

all the people I love. Over and over again. Any time we crave serious pain."

We laughed and closed up our little triangle. Standing with my arms around Jeremy and Betsy once again, I felt so lucky, so complete.

"Merry Christmas," I said. And I meant it.